EVEN A
STREET DOG

LAS VEGAS STORIES

EVEN A STREET DOG

LAS VEGAS STORIES

JOHN L. SMITH

NEVADASMITH PRESS ❖ LAS VEGAS, NEVADA

Editor: Scott Dickensheets
Designer: Sue Campbell

First Edition

ISBN: 978-0-991544-318 (print)
ISBN: 978-0-991544-325 (e-book)

 NevadaSmith Press

www.jlnevadasmith.com
Twitter: @jlnevadasmith
Email: jlnevadasmith@gmail.com
Printed in the United States of America

For Amelia

Contents

ACKNOWLEDGMENTS

The author would like to thank Cath Cassidy for her meticulous editing and unwavering belief in these little stories. The project would not have been possible without the support of Carolyn Hayes Uber of Stephens Press and former *Las Vegas Mercury* editor Geoff Schumacher. Earlier versions of many of these stories were first published in Schumacher's spirited weekly, which regrettably has faded from view.

A word about Jasper Lamar Crabbe. The name is a winking homage to the movie *Chinatown*. And like *Chinatown*, Las Vegas is a place where things are not as they seem and the conventional rules do not apply. But it is important to remember that these are works of fiction, and any similarity between the characters in these stories and living persons is a coincidence.

"Even a street dog has his lucky days."
— LI PO'S COUSIN

*"Even the dogs in the street know what
you've been up to."*
— IRISH IDIOM

PART I JASPER'S DAY OFF

WHERE YOU BEEN?

To start, a confession. When it comes to organized religion, I am a hitchhiking vagabond on the edge of an empty interstate with only the wind in the wires for company. And so I walk.

Channel surfing after another sleepless night, I land on the Religion Network, which, despite its lofty title's promise, rarely mentions more than one of the hundreds of religions that fire the hearts and spirits of billions of believers throughout the world. It is, simply, the Christian Religion Network, which nowadays takes great pains to note the biblical implications of the roaring, blood-soaked battle between the Israelis and the Palestinians and half the rest of the Arab world. It is a time in our history that should give believers great pause, a time for putting your spiritual house in order, a time for making amends with the Redeemer and spreading his Word like a sweet bird song on the spring breeze. And still I walk, listening to the hiss and sizzle of the electricity through the wires along my own private thoroughfare.

As a child of the latter-day God television, and against my best efforts, I find myself relating much of my experience to my vicarious life as a watcher. My spiritual journey, for instance, is very much like the plot line of a TV series in which Michael Landon or Grizzly Adams or

Kwai Chang Caine wanders in search of good acts and greater meaning. Problem is, life is not scripted.

My hair won't wave like Little Joe's. The bear at my side is guilt. My hands are soft and can't kick ass in the name of peace.

As I walk, I snatch a pebble from my shoe and greet the sunrise just off Main Street at Charleston Boulevard. I stand and watch the giant roaches on the wall of the pest control building and smile. A sense of nostalgia sweeps over me.

I have fond childhood memories of these roaches. The new ones are painted on; in an earlier version, the roach replicas were bolted to the building. I note the difference because this is my street, my city, my spiritual interstate.

A hitchhiker without thumbs, I wander on past Johnny Tocco's Ringside Gym up behind the sheet metal back door where the old man used to lecture pugs who were late with their dues. Back here, where one hopeless dreamer lived out of his car for most of a year while training at the gym for his professional debut, only to fold in the first round at the sight of his own blood. Back here, where the roaches are real and the spiritual men are gruff, cigar-smoking bastards who've wiped a million bloody brows. Here, where I get misty at the memories of my youth spent in the old man's cigar-fogged office, talking prospects and suspects and Mafia comings and goings.

I have to keep walking, or I'll blubber like a rummy baby. So I do, up Charleston under the train tracks where floodwater still collects deep enough to float a cabin cruiser, past the bread bakery, where the aroma at three in the morning is so intoxicating it drives hungry men to steal and others to reminisce. Past the dice clock company that could double as our crucifix factory.

It's a beautiful thing, the dice clock. It combines the bones of risk with time. It is a haiku for Las Vegas, batteries not included.

What I want more than whiskey is an epiphany, can't you tell? It is why I wander, why this story always wanders, why each piece I write takes you to another corner, into another lost life, over to the Boulevard and up to the base of the mountains and back. It is searching because I am searching through a language hopelessly infected by televised sitcom and melodrama for the right words to tell you the news. I am a Rod Sterling character with the desperate truth on my tongue's tip and seconds to go in the script.

Those lost looks in the eyes of the young? That obsession with numbers and risk? That sulfurous smell of cigarettes everywhere? Don't you get it?

I want to say, "'To Serve Man' is a cookbook," but then I reach the door of the bar and am welcomed by bug-eyed Chuck. He looks up to greet me from his vodka and video poker periscope. Out of character, he waves a round my way.

"Hey, Jasper, where you been? You look like shit. The game's on. It's Sunday morning. Let me buy you a cold one."

I nod, drink the first of many, and cut to the beer commercial that sponsors my life.

Billy Flowers, MVP

'm back downtown working graves at the El Cortez since getting out of rehab. It's a comedown from Caesars, I know, and it's a little embarrassing considering this time last year I was averaging $200 a night in tokes. That's four envelopes sometimes at the El Cortez, but I want it on the record that I appreciate the second chance. Jackie Gaughan is a man who gives a guy a second chance. Sometimes a third and fourth.

As a kid Jackie had a piece of some bookmaking parlors and card joints in Omaha. Like a lot of guys who got tired of paying off the sheriff and district attorney every four years, he moved to Las Vegas after serving a hitch in the military during World War II and opened up a store on Fremont Street. The El Cortez was a happening place in those days with Bugsy Siegel and Meyer Lansky as two of its background owners and experienced guys like Jackie running the daily action.

I think they've changed the carpet since then, but I wouldn't swear to it.

Jackie's worth maybe $200 million now. And like a man in his element, or a character out of a Dumas novel set in Vegas, he wanders the floor of the El Cortez each day in his plaid sport coat, greeting customers and employees by name, picking up empty high ball glasses and dumping overflowing ashtrays. He's a jailer who loves his jail.

The El Cortez is one of those places where business picks up the first of every month because the customers come in to cash their pension and Social Security checks, play the slots, eat a $4.95 prime rib, and forget their troubles for a few hours. You could argue that Jackie takes advantage of the Denture Cream generation, but not nearly as much as the government has by making them believe they'd have enough at the end of a life spent working to live their final years in comfort and a little dignity. Six-hundred and change a month doesn't buy you much of either, and so they wind up living next door to me in a worn out studio apartment with hopelessly urine-stained carpet and walls yellowed from the smoke of a million Lucky Strikes.

There's not a lot of money downtown anymore, but there's still a lot of good people. And, I've got to admit, a fair number of freaks. At the El Cortez, the dealers are break-in or broke-down. Even the purse-snatchers and coin cup thieves are second rate. And the customers don't know from toking or don't have much to spare after the eagle flies on Friday.

But I'll take every slack-jawed zombie and coupon-clipping piss bum on graveyard at my table before I'll deal another card to Billy Flowers. Yes, that Billy Flowers, the Major League Baseball hero who can't get into the Hall of Fame because he bet millions on sports. Mr. Baseball. Mr. MVP. The Hit Man. That Billy Flowers.

He came in here slumming the other night, and you should have heard the reaction in the pit. A genuine celebrity at the El Cortez. You'd have thought Paris Hilton danced naked on a blackjack table. It was a genuine event, a real talker in the coffee shop.

Truth is, I used to love the guy. Worshipped at his shrine, as they say. I collected his baseball cards and even became a lousy Cincinnati fan for a few seasons just to be a little closer to his greatness.

He was the fiercest ballplayer since Ty Cobb. The guy would run through brick walls to break up a double play. He'd turn bloop singles into leg doubles, would triple and slide head-first wherever he went. What was not to love?

I forgave him when he made the papers for whacking around his wife. I felt bad for him when one of his kids took a header off a 10-story building in a drug fog. I wrote him a card, but didn't know where to send it. And I argued with anyone who would listen when Major League Baseball banned him from the game that he dominated for twenty years just for making sports bets. Sure, he was betting on baseball. But did the commissioner know what a mush Flowers was? He lost millions to bookmakers and spent time in federal prison when the Internal Revenue Service caught up to him. I was his eternal enabler, as they say in the meetings.

So imagine my excitement when he emerged through blue cigarette fog to sit down at my table with a rocky road-tested blonde on his arm. He smoked a big cigar, and I could tell from the smell it was a Cuban. The whole pit looked up from the cards to watch him. The blonde giggled as she adjusted her assets.

"Hey," I said, stupidly, "you're Billy Flowers. Mr. Baseball."

"Does this mean I can get a frigging drink in this toilet?"

"Of course, Mr. Flowers," I said, embarrassed at my lack of manners. "Right away."

I barked at Maureen, who is a sweetheart but maybe the oldest cocktail waitress on Earth, to hustle up a drink for Mr. Flowers. Maureen hadn't legged out a double in many years. A piece of jerky in a polyester skirt, she spoke with the cigarette-scarred voice of a carnival-barking toad.

"What would you like, sir?" Maureen asked, showing Mr. Baseball no deference. She didn't know Billy Flowers from Billy Graham and didn't care.

"Maybe I should get up and let you sit down, Grandma," Flowers said laughing heartily. "What was it like to serve whiskey to General Grant?"

I couldn't help laughing a little, and Maureen glared at me, then focused her eyes on her tray while Billy Flowers said, "Double Chivas rocks and a Greyhound for the whore."

"Billy," the blonde whispered, stroking his arm. "Not so rough, huh?"

"I'll show you rough, sweetheart, but first I have to break the bank in this glorified Shell Station."

Maureen disappeared, and Flowers turned his attention to me. I immediately began to feel the perspiration build on my forehead. I needed a line of coke so bad I could feel it in my nostrils. Right then I would have settled for that Double Chivas. Anything to calm my nerves.

"Are you working tonight, or do I need to go to another casino?"

"No, sir. I mean, yes, sir. I'm working tonight."

"Shut up and deal," Billy Flowers said, blowing a cloud of cigar smoke in my face.

Over the next 30 minutes he abused Maureen, called the blonde a whore, and blew smoke in my face as he slowly lost three small stacks of quarter checks, which qualifies as big play at the El Cortez.

At one point I said, "We'd be glad to buy you folks a late dinner."

"Do you really think we'd eat here?" he asked. The blonde laughed nervously like a dog that had been hit a few times.

After a few hands, I retreated into that place in my head where I can think while the rest of my brain works the deck and counts the hands. I couldn't add up all the hours I'd spent thinking of Billy Flowers, all the summer days on the sandlots I'd pretended to be him running around the bases before imaginary crowds of worshipping fans.

Although I pretended not to notice, I saw that Billy had run old Maureen hard three times to the bar and hadn't dropped a chip on her tray. She wasn't awed by him when he came into the El Cortez, and she wasn't letting him under her leathered skin now.

It was me who was the coward, the coward straight out of rehab with a pansy's will power. Maureen's grace made me ashamed of being me, but so did most things.

An hour earlier I had been honored to have a member of baseball's royal family at my table. Now, with his cigar smoke making my white shirt stink like the lobby of a bus station, anger boiled up and turned my face rose-colored. Never meet your heroes in Vegas.

After losing $800, he abruptly stood up. The blonde slid off the chair and balanced on her heels. She glanced at me with thousand-mile eyes and blown-out pupils.

"Let me see one of those cards," Flowers said to me.

As whipped as the whore, I made no eye contact. But I stopped breaking down the deck and turned over a card, passing him a deuce of clubs. He pulled out a pen and signed his name, then flipped the card back across the table.

"Billy Flowers, MVP," it read.

I wanted to tell him what a Hall of Fame ass he'd made of himself, but I knew my place. In Las Vegas, knowing your place is one of the secrets of successful dealing.

My hands suddenly dripping sweat, I said, "Thank you, sir."

THE DUKE'S NEW GIRL

Because I have no life, at least not one worth detailing, I do most of my living vicariously through the Duke. I do this privately, of course. He doesn't know he's living for two. To him, I'm just Jasper the barfly, or as he sometimes calls me, "King." King Crabbe, get it?

I know I am not alone in this feeling. Charlie and Pete also are in awe of the Duke, and I suspect they, too, hurry down to Dino's early on Friday because the Duke will be there buying rounds of drinks and regaling us with stories of his week spent in the hallways of the courthouse. Of course, I don't broach the subject of my admiration for the Duke with Charlie or Pete. If by chance I was wrong and their affection for the Duke was not as great as mine, I'd never live down admitting I loved another man's life more than my own. But the truth is, I do. And they do, too.

The Duke is not a particularly handsome man. He's built like a small bear. Broad in the shoulders, broader through the middle. He's losing his hair. Outside of court, he wears a $1,000 suit with no tie, but when he enters the bar he's like Elvis in the glory years. He lights up the joint.

I look forward to Fridays with the Duke not merely because he buys the drinks, or fills us in on the latest skinny from District Court, but because it is on that day that he is most likely to be accompanied by a new girl. The Duke changes women more often than some guys change their socks. And all his girls are, shall we say, exotic.

That is why I make sure I get down to Dino's ahead of the construction workers and the Fun Book Freddies to get a good seat for the show the Duke invariably provides.

Not that all his girls are Vogue material. A few aren't fit for the cover of Popular Mechanics, but they are all incredibly smitten with the Duke.

There was one girl who flew in from California just to spend time with the Duke. I nicknamed her Muscles because she was so well built she even had developed arm muscles. The full truth is she flew in from California because she worked the baccarat bar at Caesars on the weekends, but when she was on the Duke's arm there was no confusing her loyalties. After a few drinks and pumping a few bucks through the jukebox, the Duke would tell her, "Don't just sit there, sweetheart, do a little dance."

And she'd get up and slink around like Marilyn Monroe doing "Diamonds are a Girl's Best Friend." It was pretty entertaining.

But the next time I saw the Duke he was with another girl. Judy was her name. "Judy Blue Eyes," the Duke called her. And she would say, dumb as a tuna, "They're not blue, silly, they're brown," and then shake her tail like she was scolding him.

Judy was fond of showing us her new nipple ring.

Since I'm from a generation in which women wore earrings in their ears, this came as a bit of a shock to my system. I'm no prude, mind you, but I've reached the age where I expect little more from life than a sip of whiskey and the occasional Swisher Sweet, something more exotic only if the Duke is buying.

So the nipple ring was a new one on me.

Judy also sported a tattoo of a tiger in the middle of her back and a climbing rose on her pubis. Although I can vouch for the tiger, having seen her in a halter top, I told her I would take her word for the rose. I'm a gentleman, you know. Also I'm old enough to be her grandfather.

For several months the Duke went through what I call his United Nations phase, when he dated girls who were three shades of brown as well as one Korean, one Vietnamese and one strictly of African descent. Although one of the brown girls spoke very little English and seemed painfully shy, the others were pleasant enough. And each was very attentive to the Duke.

There was a period of time he collected strippers. Again, all varieties, although strippers tend to run to the leggy, breast-enhanced and blond. Blowup dolls contain less plastic than some of the girls. They all love the Duke. He's generous with his money. But, over time a 40-watt bulb clicked on in my head. I saw that all his girlfriends made regular trips to the bathroom to fix their makeup. It was then I began to see Duke in a different light.

The Duke had really outdid himself last week. This woman was six-feet tall with a striking figure and smoldering red hair that flowed past her shoulders. She called herself Heidi and was in a class by herself. Charlie, Pete and I stopped watching the ballgame and started watching her. Like the others, she was fond of the Duke. Unlike all the rest, I noticed she still wore a wedding ring and glanced at the door often during her visit. And who can blame her?

By piecing together parts of their conversation, I learned Heidi was not only married, but wedded to Eddie Tucci, who runs a local topless bar and a string of motels that rent by the hour. Eddie Tucci is known as Little Eddie. He's also known as a connected guy with a terrible Napoleon complex.

As I know the Duke is not the marrying kind, but specializes in divorce work and arranging bail for misunderstood exotic dancers, I thought the ring and what it represented incongruous with his style. Once I discovered Heidi's true identity, I was reminded that love in Las Vegas can be a dangerous thing.

Not that it is my place to question his judgment in barroom affairs of the heart. His expertise in such areas is unparalleled among his peers.

It's not easy to find love in the city. That's what makes the Duke so special. He seems to find it everywhere he looks.

But in light of current events, I find myself thankful for my own small life. I've decided I no longer want to live through the Duke at all.

Coltrane Heart

read somewhere the other day that scientists believe music and noises from Earth can escape the atmosphere and travel in radio waves through space. That way, one day the Man in the Moon or Martians or whoever is out there will be standing out in a field somewhere and hear the voice of Sinatra or the Beatles or some idiot reading the ball scores.

I am not convinced it flies away, but I know some music stays way inside people, right in their bones and blood. At least it was that way with Charlie.

Charlie's dead now. He died of heroin and a broken heart. I knew him as a barfly late in his life when he was reduced to acting as a glorified Western Union boy for a local drug dealer.

How Charlie died is another story, and the murder of his girlfriend, Sweet Thing, can wait, too. Today I want to tell about the time Charlie told me the truth about the nature of his love and his madness.

It was late September. The valley was rocked by thunder and lightning, the storm full of heat and wind and gray foreboding, but no rain. Charlie stepped in out of the afternoon and took a seat next to me at Atomic Liquors.

Charlie talked in rhyme and bursts of patter. At times his rhyme was pure doggerel, but occasionally he seemed inspired. Sometimes he would repeat himself for dramatic effect. For instance, when one of the local thug soldiers would enter the bar and flash a menacing glare, Charlie would say, "This cat, this cat, this cat, this cat Shaft is a baaaad muthafuckah" and laugh until he nearly pissed himself.

On the afternoon he showed me his heart, I realized that what was going on inside him wasn't a simple tale of ordinary madness, but something those astronomers might have found fascinating. His inner being buzzed with heroin and the rhythms of John Coltrane.

Sweet Thing had left him again, and his worldly possessions did not fill half the hefty sack that squatted at his feet.

"Free again?" I asked, my eyes taking in the sack and his face.

"Free to be, free to see, free to feel the real."

"Too real," I said, and he nodded.

It was then he explained how his life was not about drugs, but about lost love. As I listened he sounded like a Poe character who had searched for El Dorado but had wound up with a sack of dirty laundry and a blistering addiction.

In other words, like most of us when you really think about it. It was then he mentioned Coltrane.

"I am his horn," Charlie said. "As I was born and heard the sound, sound, sound of Coltrane's music, a young cat

digs his sound and lives forever more, his art in my heart.
A love supreme, I have a dream, his dream."

And then he proposed a toast.

"To his birthday and mine."

"Whose birthday and yours?

"My spirit, my saint. Can't you hear it? It's faint."

He looked askance, then patted my shoulder.

"He plays 'My Favorite Things,' his saxophone sings,
inside my brain, each refrain whispers his name, John
Coltrane."

"I didn't know you were musical, Charlie," I said.

"I'm an artist who performs in dreams, lives well in
dreams, loves righteously in dreams, stands tall in dreams,
sees all in dreams. It's only when I awake that it all turns
to mud. It's in my blood."

Charlie told me his life's goal was to be Coltrane. He
believed they were linked cosmically because their birth-
days were the same. Charlie put down his tenor for good
on July 17, 1967, the day Coltrane died in Huntington,
Long Island.

"Since then I dream in Coltrane, speak in Coltrane, live
for Coltrane. I am the light, the dark, the blues, the lark,
the hues and spark, a disciple of the heart. Oh Lord my
joy is as pain, for each day I'm chasing the Trane. I'm
Afro-Blue and Blue Trane, Round Midnight I'm Walkin'
on Green Dolphin Street. I'm sweet for Cousin Mary and
dream of Rev. King and the Cosmos of a Love Supreme."

Charlie wasn't just babbling. He'd been reciting songs
his hero had recorded. The arrangements played over
and over in his head.

I listened awhile longer, then rose to leave and took a walk in the electrical storm, thinking there must be something to that theory that music keeps traveling.

GINGER AND THE TWINS

When Ginger first started tending bar at the Beer Barrel Tavern, the regulars immediately warmed up to her. She was easy to like. Ginger was built like a boy but swaggered like a Navy sailor. She wasn't afraid to cuss a little and on occasion told a naughty joke, but for the most part she was all class and only flirted with the patrons whose days of rutting had gone out with the Eisenhower administration.

Ginger was one of the guys, and she smiled when they nicknamed her Ginger Snap. It seemed to suit her sassy personality. Once in a while a smart guy would come up with "How about an ale, Ginger, not a ginger ale, get it?" But mostly they just called her Ginger Snap.

Although she was friendly to the fellow at the bar, it was clear to astute observers that Ginger wasn't in the market for a date with any of the usual suspects. Truth is, about the time she took the job her girlfriend, Laura, started coming in regularly.

It was no big deal to me, and anyone who might have noticed the two occasionally make eye contact through the haze of cigarette smoke never said a word. I'd had several pleasant conversations with Laura, a local UPS driver. In time, she, too, became one of the guys.

The wheel of life being what it is, I spent a few months in cocktail lounges across town and missed Ginger's transformation, but even a man of my advanced age noticed the difference the first time I set foot back in the Beer Barrel one early afternoon. Ginger had changed.

"We call 'em the Twins," Chuck the Realtor said, as proudly as if they were his own.

They being the set of back-breaking breast implants that Ginger sported.

"She looks like a snake that swallowed a set of cannon balls," the Corporal whispered, conspiratorially.

Added Butch, "We're thinking of changing her nickname to Ginger Grant. You know, like the chick from Gilligan's Island."

I could see they'd been concentrating long and hard on the new development in Ginger's life.

Personally, I'm not a big fan of the Vegas Android babes who get their breasts super-inflated, their ribs shaved, noses whittled and chins rebuilt. It makes me wonder what's going on inside their heads that they're so uncomfortable with their appearance that they resort to a fortune in plastic surgery.

Ginger, for instance, was as flat as a dollar bill but had a helluva personality. Anyone who would judge her by her bra size alone wouldn't have been worth her time, I figured, but then I'd been out of the dating game a few years.

I took a seat and in a moment Ginger was front and center in a halter top and unbuttoned vest. At least, I assume she'd unbuttoned the vest. It was possible the buttons had popped off.

"What can I get you, Jasper honey?" she asked. "Long time no see."

"A tequila and a draft, thanks," I said. "Have you changed your hair style?"

I smiled. She smiled.

"Guess again," she said, waving her chest my way.

For a moment I thought she'd fall over. But she righted herself, and out of the corner of my eye I noticed her friend, Laura, taking it all in.

Within thirty minutes, the Beer Barrel began to change. The usual crowd was suddenly awash in twenty-something junior executives and construction workers, all edging and angling their way up to the bar for a drink and a gander at the Twins. Ginger took a long stretch at the cash register, yawned at the Budweiser tap, and leaned into every paying customer.

By the time Happy Hour ended she was sweeping greenbacks off the bar top and filling her tip spittoon to overflowing. And all the while her friend said not a word.

When the crowd thinned out again I ordered another drink and said, "So, tell me, what's the difference at the bottom line between now and three months ago?"

"I average three times the tips and 10 times the marriage proposals," Ginger said.

"And they don't know about Laura?" I asked.

"That would spoil all the fun, don't you think?" Ginger replied.

"Your secret's safe with me, my dear," I told her, patting her hand and trying not to blush.

THE REAL McCoy

I saw Tony Marino the other day, but not in the usual place.
He wasn't sipping vodka over ice at Piero's in his
$2,000 Brioni with a $7,500 Rolex and diamond pinkie
ring glittering in the lounge light. He was behind the
wheel of a ten-year-old Chevy pickup with Tony's Lawn
Care painted in block letters on the door.

Those who know the reputation of Tony and his
younger brother, Tommy, will appreciate the incongruity of the sight. The Marino brothers being the princes
of the city's wannabe wiseguys and all.

In addition to being known for its casinos and big
hotels, Las Vegas is the wannabe wiseguy capital of the
world. There are more matinee mobsters here per capita
than anywhere outside Hollywood. If all the mopes in
Las Vegas who acted like connected guys were the real
McCoy, organized crime would have more members than
the Republican Party. But it's not that way.

As a rule of thumb, Las Vegas has a thousand wan-
nabes for every connected guy, and about fifty connected
guys for every made guy. Although they still manage to
get things done on the street, there aren't enough active
made guys in Las Vegas to fill a short school bus.

It's not that the poseurs aren't dangerous. On the contrary. Many are more bloodthirsty than Scarface Al. But they're complete cowboys, which is to say extremely undisciplined, and that makes them magnets for law enforcement and unreliable in a pinch.

Tony and Tommy Marino came from good stock. Their papa was connected and their Uncle Dominic was made. But the bloodline messed up somewhere.

Perhaps they were doomed from the start. Their trouble was simple: They watched too much television and volunteered for work they weren't prepared for. That's how they almost got killed by a rival outfit, the toughest mob in the history of Las Vegas. Got out by the skin of their tails, as it were.

It happened a few years ago that a local grind joint operator named Sid Ross had fallen behind on an arrangement he'd made with Anthony Spilotro, who was a genuine, all-American, gun-toting tough guy, now deceased. As Tony was being watched by a rival gang, he decided to do a favor for Rocky Marino and put his kids to work canceling Sid Ross's debt permanently.

Ross knew how unhealthy it was falling behind on a deal with the Little Guy. Instead of running away, he became a snitch for the Metro Intelligence Bureau. Turning rat was dangerous, but standing around waiting for Spilotro to lose his patience was worse. So when Ross spotted the Marinos skulking around like a couple of extras from The Godfather, Part III, he phoned his friends at the police department.

The Las Vegas mob cops did what they did best in those days, namely load their weapons and set up an ambush. They didn't have long to wait.

After two nights sitting in the dark at Sid's home, the cops were rewarded. The Marinos slipped a shiv into the backdoor jamb and cracked the lock. The detectives waited a count of three, then opened up. What, you were expecting "Come out with your hands up?" No such luck. In those days, the Constitution didn't apply to wiseguys.

Two detectives fired seventeen times in the dark and ruined Sid's living room. Blew up his TV set, even. The Marinos were on the ground, wetting their pants and loudly professing their passivity. They went from would-be hitmen to conscientious objectors in under ten seconds, a new record.

The physical damage was surprisingly slight. Only Tony had been hit, and he sustained a flesh wound up the butt. Tommy was hit only by the Holy Spirit as he thanked the Blessed Trinity for his miraculous good fortune. They both pleaded guilty to burglary and weapons charges, served under three years of penitentiary time, and returned to Las Vegas.

Then a strange thing happened. Instead of returning to their places as bookend bulldogs at Piero's or Cafe Michelle, they stopped hanging out in all the usual places. Instead, Tommy got a job as a clerk in a Smith's Food King and Tony, with his permanent limp, stopped cutting up and turned to cutting grass. They occasionally put their heads together and pulled a burglary or drug dealer extortion, but their days as social climbing connected criminals was over.

They had almost been done in by the meanest mob ever to walk the streets of Las Vegas, the one whose members carry a badge and keep their pistols in plain sight.

Dangerous Roll

I've always been a big newspaper reader. I pore over the headlines and ball scores with a zeal I once had for the female form. But as I've grown older I have learned to enjoy a juicy Las Vegas news story more than the shapeliest figure. It may sound crazy, but wait until you're old. You'll see.

There are few things I like better than to spread out my papers at a cafe or hole-in-the-wall Mexican restaurant and read the daily news. With that in mind, imagine my surprise as I sat amid the stacks of newsprint at the El Sombrero the other day, slurping a bowl of chili verde and reading the news article featuring my second wife, Cassandra Prophet.

Cassandra, a former principal dancer at the Lido and former co-host of a late-night horror movie series on local television, had been arrested in the shooting death of her husband, Sol Bernstein of Bernstein's Steam & Press fame. He is the guy who for years did his own TV sales pitches: "I'm Sol Bernstein and I'm steeeeeeeaming over the high price of dry cleaning."

I nearly spilled my chili. Cassandra had let the steam out of Sol with three shots in the chest from a snub-nosed

.357. "Self-defense," she told arresting officers. "Tight grouping," I say.

Cassandra and I were married for eight weeks many years ago during a time I believed my luck and youth would last forever. Having lived in Las Vegas for so long, I should have known better.

At that time in my life, luck was the easy part. I was winning every baseball bet I made, laying off for three out-of-town bookmakers, and was streaking at the blackjack tables. I had more money than I knew what to do with.

Then I met Cassandra. She just sort of appeared next to me while I was busy separating the Horseshoe from a great many of its black chips. She was clearly someone's shill, and I presumed the house had sent her over to keep an eye on me, but I couldn't help being flattered. Oh, Lord, but she was a handsome thing. Nearly six-feet tall, blond hair, a sensational smile. What startled me about her were her dark eyes. They were probably just dark brown, but they seemed black as the chips I was piling in front of me. When she smiled, they did not. I should have taken that as a sign then, but my youth was getting in the way.

I bet for her, and of course she won. I took her home and thought I'd found the meaning of life. In two weeks we were married.

In retrospect, I think my luck changed that night. She moved in, my bankroll dropped like a penny stock, and within two weeks she'd managed to run up two credit cards in my name that I didn't even know I had.

Then came the night I told her no more, that I wasn't
made of money. She nodded and said, "Maybe you aren't,
lover, but I am."

She made a phone call, left the apartment I had at the
Las Vegas Country Club, was gone for three days.

In that time, I won thirteen of seventeen plays and
could feel my focus return. As if drawn to the money,
Cassandra returned and immediately attempted to rekindle
our romance. When I reminded her of a few rules, she
snapped at me. By the time she left a week later, she'd
found my getaway money in a shoebox in the back of
my closet and had drained a bank account I was sure no
one knew about. I swear the woman could smell money.

When I tracked her down, I found her on the arm
of a connected guy in a quiet lounge at Caesars. When
I approached the table, she opened her beaded purse
wide enough to reveal the pistol she carried with her.
She whispered to her bulldog boyfriend, who snarled
and stood up. I barely noticed him, but couldn't help
getting a chill as I looked into her dark, flat eyes. They
were the eyes of a shark.

The bulldog expected trouble, but instead I reached
out my hand. In shock, he shook mine.

"Congratulations," I said. "You must be very happy."

I spun on my heel, wrote off the losses, and changed
the numbers on my phone, credit cards and bank account.
In a few days my luck returned, and I spent the heat of
the Las Vegas summer at Del Mar, managing my money
with my face into the cool ocean breeze.

After finishing the story on Cassandra, I made a few bets and went to bed early. Before sleep came, I tried to picture her as a gorgeous twenty-five-year-old and me on a dangerous roll. All I could think of were those shark eyes. I went to bed with a relatively clear conscience and a nagging pain in the middle of my chest.

It was probably the chili.

Double D

I never missed a Don Dias column. For years he was known as the best columnist in the city, a real street-guy-turned-newsman who was unafraid to take on politicians and the hoodlum element. Those in the know swore by him. Some wiseguys I know swore at him.

He's dead now. He died of a heart attack while on vacation in the tropics as the guest of a certain well-connected guy in town. Not that such a fact made print, for no one in the local media world would dream of besmirching Don's legend.

I hadn't known him two minutes before I realized what it was about him that made people want to spill their secrets. He wasn't a tall man, or devilishly handsome, and in the early days he always wore a cheap cotton oxford shirt with a stained tie slip-knotted around his neck. He was a character who was well-read and had a sense of humor. He instilled in the people he met a sense of trust and confidence, the sort usually reserved for family members and best friends.

Don got drunk one night at a local topless joint I frequented in my younger days and dropped his wallet. I found it, returned it to him, and we struck up a friendship.

"Here's to The Last Honest Man," he'd greet me with a crooked grin as I came through the door of Rube's or Irene's or half a dozen other places.

"Here's to Double D," which is what I called him. He liked the name. It fit his image and his penchant for heavy-chested women.

"Jasper, my friend, if you ever catch me becoming one of those establishment assholes, give me a slap," Don would say after the Scotch kicked in. "A newsman in this town has to be his own man, or he's no man at all. This town will suck the heart out of you if you're not careful."

"I'm sure you'll stay straight as a string," I replied.

With a few variations, we had that conversation often in the years we were on speaking terms. Don was rightly concerned that the real Las Vegas House edge would grind him down and turn him into another trick pony for a handful of powerful men. He'd seen it happen to others similarly situated.

The real House edge here isn't a mathematical advantage at blackjack or craps. It's the atmosphere, the booze, party girls and lack of clocks. For a human being trying to stay straight, it's maybe impossible to beat. I've seen plenty of square apples come to town with an iron-clad set of morals and beliefs and watched them turn into bug-eyed video poker freaks overnight. And even the strongest sexual constitution can turn to Jell-O when confronted with a willing set of surgically enhanced ta-tas.

There are times I think Las Vegas exists to subjugate women and ruin men. But Don seemed to be the exception to the rule. I believed that even after I saw him driving around town in a fine foreign automobile that had been leased by a local advertising firm. I continued to believe it even after I saw him win the easy favor of a string of strippers who appeared to have been provided by a local topless club operator.

I guess I stopped believing it the night he sidled up to me with that crooked grin and a gutful of booze, ordered me a round, then brushed up against me and pointed to the cuff of a new shirt he was wearing.

"Check this out, Jasper my man," he said. "A monogrammed shirt, tailor-made. It's made of silk. Pretty nice, huh?"

"Very nice, Donnie," I said. "You buy that yourself, did you? News business pays better than I thought."

"I can afford it," he said. "I got this consulting deal with a couple companies in town, and I'm doing some freelancing. It adds up."

"Apparently," I said. "I'll bet it took a lot of worms to make that silk shirt."

He laughed.

"And talented ones, too," Don Dias said.

"How's that?"

"From the look of the monogram," he said, "they even knew my name."

I never did slap old Double D like he'd wanted me to. By then it was too late. The House had won again.

Cost of Living

Only a few years ago, if you asked me to find the Professor, I'd know right where to look. He'd be camped on a bar stool at the old Philly Pub drinking draft beer, chain-smoking, pumping quarters into a video poker machine, and offering his expert opinion on a variety of subjects to anyone willing to listen.

In those days, a lot of people did listen to the Professor. He was considered something of an intellect around the valley. In a community full of drugstore cowboys, working-class wiseguys, lamisters and losers, he was something of an anomaly: a university-certified phenomenon.

When I first met him he was known in the press as the "Baby-Faced Professor" because he held the distinction of being the youngest recipient of a Ph.D. in the history of the University of Nevada System. Not only that, but he had a face that could have passed for 14 or 15. For years he got carded at bars and always took umbrage.

His doctoral thesis was titled Applied Mathematical Theory in Modern Gaming. He was in his early twentiess and wrote his lengthy dissertation about the time the rest of his friends were coming back from Vietnam. He received several big job offers out of state and one at the local university, but decided to stay in Las Vegas and teach in public school. He was giving something back

45

where his gifts could do the most good, he announced, and people were impressed. He took a job at his alma mater, Las Vegas High. He married a local girl, had three ordinary children, and every school day insisted students address him as doctor.

That was nearly thirty-five years ago. Since then, the Professor had made a number of changes in his life.

He had changed offices many times, but nothing about his behavior. Since then he'd been tossed out of Skinny Dugan's twice, the Rice Paddy, Tap House, Trap House, Four Kegs, Triple Play twice, Andy Capz and Decatur Liquor three separate times. It seemed not everyone appreciated the Professor's expert opinion as much as he enjoyed giving it.

People are funny sometimes. I, for one, prefer my liquor without so much learning. I like to read the newspaper and drink beer in the corner of a well-lighted bar, but I leave the textbooks and pop quizzes at home. Not so the Professor.

Time had changed everything but his expert opinion, and it made me wonder whether education is all it's cracked up to be.

Through the years the Professor exchanged draft beer for vodka tonics, the first wife and family for a second and third marriage. He had traded his home for a condo and the condo for a studio apartment. And through it all he hadn't missed a video poker payment. His tenacious consistency in that regard was truly remarkable. Perhaps he was still working on his theory.

He had also exchanged that photogenic fresh face for a deeply creased scowl, a vein-riddled, oversized nose, squinting hawk eyes and a nasty nicotine hack. But those of us still standing have all changed plenty in thirty-five years.

Recently I stepped into Pogo's for a draft beer after a long walk and found the Professor at the bar being waited on by Mary, the sweetheart who had come to Las Vegas to hear the big band music and never left. Pogo's is the city's quintessential hole-in-the-wall with Dixieland jazz on Friday nights and drafts for under a buck. Its regulars are friendly, but I seldom go there because of the soft lighting and my newspaper-reading habit. The number of patrons at the bar compelled me to sit next to the Professor, and class commenced as soon as I did.

In ten minutes I learned about the cynical world of Washington politics, the uselessness of maintaining a religious belief system in an era in which, clearly, TV was God, and then something really useful: The Professor was leaving Las Vegas for good. I nearly choked.

"Las Vegas has changed forever, not for better I fear," the Professor said, looking up from the glow of his poker machine. "It was possible to exist in a cultural wasteland so long as the cost of living was favorable. Economics wins out over aesthetics every time. But now the cost of living in Las Vegas is too great."

I had a last look at the Baby-Faced Professor in that inferior light, decided to him at his word and not ask if there were poker machines where he was moving.

ME AMERICA

Many locals have their favorite casino, and one or two they simply refuse to set foot in, but my insomnia does not discriminate. Although I have a special affinity for downtown's grind joints, a given year will find me visiting casinos grand and diminutive at least once. Unlike some, who prefer fresh air and blissful silence, I thrive on the cigarette haze and jarring slot jangle of the gambling joints.

With one exception.

It's a popular casino marketed to locals, one with a snappy theme song and commercials featuring bikini-clad dancers. It's not the treatment I've received that keeps me away from there like a haunted mansion. Nor is it the food. Fact is, the joint is a fine place to spend a few hours of the time I have left on Earth.

It's Mr. Ng's voice that haunts me even after three years.

I met him as I meet so many acquaintances on the street, by making eye contact and saying thank you when he poured me a cup of coffee in the cafe. He was an exceedingly polite gentleman, whose uniform was pressed and adorned with a tiny American flag pin. His employee tag read, "Hi I'm Jimmy from America."

Mr. Ng. was so small and slender he could have been an apprentice jockey had his face not betrayed him. It was lined and cut as if shaped by a century of wind and rain. I am generally a good judge of age, but was at a loss with Mr. Ng. He could have been fifty, or eighty.

In time, I would notice that he had no fingernails, just knots of white scar tissue. It did not prevent him from serving meals and pouring coffee, but after I'd gotten to know him he smiled sheepishly and said, "I come to Vegas to learn deal cards. Fingers not work enough. No feel card. So waiter now. Me America. Everything good."

As I made a point of returning to his area, we began to make small talk. Mr. Ng always greeted me with a smile and a fresh cup of coffee. Despite his weathered face and smoky dark eyes, he was a joyous little man.

"Where are you from originally, Mr. Ng?" I asked one morning between bites of breakfast.

When he returned to my table he said, "Little Sapa. Small village. My hometown. But now me America. Everything good."

Sapa, as I eventually discovered, was located in Vietnam near the northern Chinese border. It was home to many Hmong people, whose fathers and sons fought alongside American troops in Vietnam. With my factoid memorized, I returned to find Mr. Ng and report what I had learned.

"Very good, Mr. Jasper," he replied with a smile, making a marvelous mispronunciation of my name. I didn't mind. Here was a good man making his way in the world.

"You are Hmong, no?" I asked.

He nodded.

"Hmong, yes. You know Hmong? Good people, Hmong. Good friend, America."

"Very brave people, I think," I said.

Mr. Ng smiled a little.

"Me America now," Mr. Ng said. "Live large. Got house. Good days ahead."

For nearly a year we conversed as waiter and customer before I invited him for coffee. To my surprise, he accepted, but only on Saturday afternoon at one p.m. It was, I discovered, the hour a week he kept to himself from his two jobs and family. He wore a suit to tea at a Denny's near my place downtown.

And he gave me a gift, a small poem written in his native language on the thinnest paper. It was wrapped in a bright piece of cloth that appeared to be handmade. Embarrassed, I insisted on buying the tea.

Of course I couldn't understand the poem, so he translated.

"'Risk all things for free dreams,' it say," Mr. Ng said.

A younger man would have been smug enough to say he knew what Mr. Ng meant, but I could only imagine what he had risked. He looked me in the eye and read my mind.

"Me America now," he said. "Got no worry."

• • •

In the time I was acquainted with Mr. Ng, I cannot say I knew him well. Our language barrier was one reason. His war experiences were another.

Try as he might, his English was halting. It was, of course, far superior to my Vietnamese, but his limited vocabulary kept the topics of conversation simple, somewhat superficial and often in the present tense.

It was in the present tense that he mentioned in passing that his fingers had been mangled during the war after he was captured by the enemy. The enemy of America, he said. He wasn't complaining, only explaining why he could not deal cards for a living.

If he was very interested in my stories of life in Las Vegas before the corporate titans seized the street and began wringing gold from the grind joints at a rate never dreamed of by the mob, it did not show much on his face. He was always polite and almost studious in his contemplation and inevitable follow-up question, but his inquiries were limited. In response to what I considered an inspired monologue about the importance of Moe Dalitz to the history of the town, Mr. Ng would reply with something like, "So, Moe Dalitz a good man, not a bad man?"

He was right, of course. In his consummate simplicity he had captured the never-ending question that haunts all of the founding fathers of Las Vegas. Where they came from, they were bad men. Some were rum-runners and gamblers. Others were cold-blooded killers without a trace of conscience. But once they crossed the desert, unpacked their bags, shuffled up and paid their taxes, they became good men. They were reborn in the middle of nowhere like a bunch of back-page biblical figures.

"Las Vegas good," Mr. Ng said. "Las Vegas good to me like Moe Dalitz."

I smiled at the notion that this kind, gentle, poem-writing man no larger than a jockey would compare himself to Dalitz, who despite his small stature was one of the biggest men in Las Vegas history. Dalitz had managed to build much of the Strip in the era before a self-respecting bank would loan Las Vegas gamblers a nickel. Dalitz had been in on the ground floor of the Desert Inn, the Stardust and other resorts. He'd been the driving force behind the construction of the Las Vegas Country Club, which would not only allow Jews to become members but would encourage them to participate in an atmosphere many had been forbidden to enjoy in their home cities. Dalitz helped develop the first privately owned hospital, the first major shopping mall, the first planned golf course community.

Dalitz bankrolled the business careers of some of the community's biggest names, some of whom later downplayed his influence on their lives. He also made political careers with a well-timed contribution or a simple pat on the back. He was Southern Nevada's godfather in the best sense of the word.

Mr. Ng was a Hmong from Sapa who served coffee and took short orders from tourists and guys like me. It was only after he was gone that I realized what he'd meant.

I was in the cafe when the FBI agents in their gray suits entered and flanked him, placing their hands on his shoulders with casino security and two Metro officers looking on. He did not struggle. There was clearly no use. He set his coffee pot down and submitted to their wishes, placing his hands behind his back in full view of the other customers.

For a moment I saw Mr. Ng. He waved his crippled hands.

"Me America," he was telling the agents, who clearly weren't listening. "Me good friend, America. Loyal and true."

He began to mumble almost incoherently. I was incensed.

"What's the meaning of this?" I asked. "What has he done?"

"He's under arrest for smuggling human beings," a cop said. "It's a federal thing. Apparently he's part of an organization that's responsible for shipping hundreds of illegals here from China."

"Vietnam," I said. "Mr. Ng is from Vietnam."

"Well," the smart-ass cop replied, "he'll be returning there shortly."

I followed him all the way out through the side entrance of the casino, where the agents placed him in the back of a tan Buick. I approached the glass and one FBI man rolled down the window.

Before I could speak I heard Mr. Ng say, "Please help, Mr. Jasper. Me America. Risk all things, free dreams."

I wanted to shout, but the cry caught in my throat. What could an old man do but watch him go?

PONYTAIL

The last time I'd seen Bobby Boyd in person, as opposed to on one of his television commercials, he was still making a killing in Las Vegas real estate. He was several years younger and a far better hustler. In just a few years he'd gone from a mediocre dice dealer when we worked together at Caesars to the man who proclaimed himself "Your Local Connection in the Las Vegas home market."

Boyd Realty made a big name for itself, and for many years Bobby was very successful and enjoyed the usual trappings of wealth. But, as most Americans know, wealth means little without celebrity.

There was something about the commercials he produced that, at least in his mind, made him a celebrity. Who could reasonably say otherwise? He was on television, the place movie stars delivered their lines and won canned laughter. His face was more recognized than the governor's. He was stopped often on the street and in restaurants, and people sometimes pointed at him during UNLV basketball games and big boxing matches. Those commercials, which weren't all that bad, made him into a popular household name around Southern Nevada.

Around his own household, his name was decidedly less popular. Bobby partied his way out of two marriages. He found early on that one place he appeared to be very well recognized was at the local topless cabarets, where the girls often smiled and asked him if he was "looking for a connection." He got a kick out of being singled out, and over time he came to expect such special treatment. Not only from strippers, but from waiters, auto mechanics and local bureaucrats.

After a few drinks, the truth came out. Bobby got bored with real estate. It didn't challenge him. He had to admit he'd pretty much mastered the game locally, made good money and better investments in the mortgage-lending racket. He was secure, but uninspired. And as a creative person, one reason he'd insisted on appearing in—and then writing and producing—his own commercials had been to feed his creative hunger. He needed an outlet. Some people couldn't understand that.

Boyd Realty eventually went bankrupt, but from the look of things at Starbucks Bobby was still doing all right for himself. Where my own hair had thinned and gone gray, his had darkened considerably. He wore a ponytail, sunglasses and a Florida tan. The morning was chilly, but his shirt was wide open at the collar.

He'd pulled up in a silver Mercedes convertible and was accompanied by a tall brunette who wore too much makeup for perhaps eighteen. She was very shapely, that much was clear, and the straps of her frilly brassiere were exposed by the cut of her T-shirt. My eyes haven't lost all their ability to focus.

She ordered the tallest, creamiest, most caramelized coffee drink in the house. It looked like a milkshake. He sipped a cup of espresso, looked detached, fiddled with his ponytail. As I have reached that age where I've become an anonymous old man, he didn't recognize me when they sat down at the adjacent table. How could he? I'd aged while he'd gotten younger.

"Normally, Tiffany, I like to meet with an agent first to make sure all the paperwork is in order, but since you're a close friend of Jerry's I figured you were a serious actor looking for work," Bobby said.

"Exactly, Mr. Boyd," she said. "Acting is what I've wanted to do my whole life."

"First, call me Bobby. Second, I have two projects in the works, and I might be able to use someone like you," he said. "You'll have to read for the parts, of course, but we can arrange that."

"I'm ready when you are," she said.

"Have you ever seen When Harry Met Sally?" he asked, a grin dripping from his face. His teeth had been capped. "Remember the deli scene?"

Suddenly eighteen going on forty-five, she smiled.

"You don't want me to try that here, do you?"

"Heavens no, sweetheart. You'll give the older customers cardiac arrest."

She laughed.

"You're so funny," she said. "I like that in a man."

"You know what I like in a woman?" he asked.

"I think I can guess," she said.

With that, he finished his espresso and stood, reaching out his hand. She took her milkshake to go.

As I watched them leave, I wondered what had become of all the young, handsome girls of my Las Vegas youth.

AMONG GHOSTS

couldn't sleep again, but instead of sitting in the dark listening to AM radio signals from distant lands I got dressed and went into the night to meet a few acquaintances I suspect have been dead for years.

Not dead in the medical sense. Their hearts are beating. To the casual observer they function almost normally. But if I didn't know better, I'd swear they were sleepwalking, or worse.

At first I chalked it up to the effects of drugs and drinking on them and me. Although the younger generation loves to experiment with each new designer drug that is brewed in a trailer in San Bernardino County or body-packed up from Mexico, alcohol remains the undisputed heavyweight champion of drugs. It's a candy mint, it's a breath mint. It's safe and effective when used as directed.

In Las Vegas, you can get it twenty-four hours a day.

Alcohol. Ask for it by name.

But mere inebriation doesn't explain this late-night phenomenon. And I have learned after many long years of research that it's not tied to one cocktail lounge or toilet tavern.

That is to say, there is no one dive that is best for channeling ghosts. It's just something that happens, or at least something that has been happening to me lately.

I can't sleep, decide to get dressed and go for a walk, which is my battered conscience's way of telling me it's okay to have a drink at three a.m. Get up, throw a little water on my face, check my look in the mirror. Gray as a gym sock, wrinkled as an old apple.

Too old to hit on, too young for Depends, I move almost invisibly from place to place. Although I consider myself an above-average toker, bartenders care not a bit whether I tip generously or not at all. To them, I am merely a lonely old man.

Customers sitting near me avoid eye contact. I was young once. I know what they're thinking: "Old guy alert. If I acknowledge his existence, he'll want to talk about Clinton, his VA benefits or why baseball was better in the dead-ball era." But they are wrong. If I wanted to carry on a conversation with a young person, I would have stayed home and talked to the TV set.

Unless it is to unlock the ghost, I don't want to speak at all. I want to listen.

I was at the Ukelele Lounge sipping my usual and testing my theory when a ghost came in and took a seat next to me. She was perhaps thirty or sixty-five, it was difficult to tell. One thing was certain, she was not of this world. As I listened I heard her carrying on a conversation with her mother, who was clearly deceased.

"Don't tell me I told you so, Mama," she said above the din of booze-blistered voices, staring blankly toward the back bar. "I'm no fool. Do you think I don't know what day it is? I can take care of my own kitty, thank you very much."

She was so convincing that for a moment I presumed she wasn't speaking a euphemism and fought the urge to look for the cat. In a while, she returned to her conversation.

"Soup is my favorite, Mama. Tomato soup. With cream in it like you make. That soup so good. When you gonna make me that soup again? I'm hungry, Mama, so hungry for your soup. Kitty doesn't like the soup, Mama, but she sure likes the cream. Sweet kitty, where'd she go? Have you seen her, Mama? I know you don't think I can take care of my own kitty, but I can, I know I can. She so soft and fine. Scratchy tongue and tiny wet nose. Sweet kitty, where you been?"

In a few minutes, the bartender came over to her and said, "You gotta go. Shoo now."

She looked up astonished.

"But what about my kitty?"

"I haven't seen your kitty, Mary. Not tonight, not last night, not last week. You gotta go now."

Through the haze of cigarette smoke I saw tears in her eyes. She rose from her bar stool, glided toward the door and was gone. I left two coins on the bar and followed her outside.

I don't move as quickly as I once did but made good time, hitting the door only seconds behind her. I didn't know what I was going to say to her when I found her, but I'd think of something.

When I got outside I expected to bump into her, but instead found the littered parking lot empty. A car coming from downtown ran a red light and vanished down

Las Vegas Boulevard into Northtown. Crazy Mary was gone. Really gone, and I wasn't hallucinating.

Since then I have catalogued dozens of ghost sightings, all of which share a few elements in common. Although they often speak, their dialogue is clearly internal in nature. They are capable of understanding others, but incapable of carrying on a conversation above the voice in their head. The subject are sometimes docile, sometimes appear dangerous, often have visions, rarely order a drink, always appear to be seeking an answer that never comes.

I know what you're thinking. Not only does that describe half the population, but it's textbook schizophrenia. Ordinary crazy. Maybe.

That doesn't explain the Houdini act, does it?

Since noticing the phenomenon, all but three of these ghosts have vanished before I reach the door. I mean disappeared.

Anyone can do this research, but I don't recommend floating among the ghosts of Las Vegas. It's strictly for insomniacs and those who must wander the night.

In those late hours, I feel half alive myself.

Cormorant Luck

As a younger man, I drove everywhere. But as my eyesight has worsened and my body has slowed down, I enjoy getting out and walking. Somehow, when I'm breathing in fresh air and feeling my legs work it makes me feel a little more alive.

Except when it's cold.

These days I am often surprised by how the changes in temperature affect me. It was in the fifties the other day when I arrived at Lorenzi Park for a Sunday walk around the lake, but it may as well have been freezing.

I made it halfway around before my knees began to ache, then decided to take a break on a park bench and bask like an old lizard in the winter sun. The lake is really little more than a pond brimming with algae-green water and dotted with mud hens and ornery geese. But in Las Vegas you take your nature where you find it.

It was then I noticed the cormorants in the leafless branches of a cottonwood tree, black apparitions against a steel-blue sky. From afar, the long-necked fish ducks could have been quarter notes on a giant sheet of music.

I'd never seen cormorants in a tree before. They are renowned as the birds trained by the Chinese to fish with a metal band around their slender necks to prevent them from swallowing their catch. I was soaking up the sunshine and thinking of how different things are in some cultures, when a disheveled fellow sat at the far end of the bench. He was much younger than me, but that's true of almost everyone I meet.

Still, I recognized his face despite the shaggy beard. It was Ricky Billings, who had stormed onto the high-stakes Las Vegas poker scene by winning the World Championship of Hold 'Em in his first tournament. The press loved him because he had graduated with honors in mathematics from the Massachusetts Institute of Technology. The columnists called him "Young Einstein," and his opponents called him "The Savant." He took home a million dollars and appeared on the *Letterman* show.

Two years later, Billings made headlines again when he was featured on *60 Minutes* in an investigative piece on the mobsters who bankrolled some of the world's best gamblers. Ricky Billings was one of several young math geniuses who had been bankrolled by men associated with organized crime.

Overnight Billings became notorious. Within six months he was nominated for inclusion in Nevada's Black Book. If he wanted to fight it, it didn't show. He didn't bother to appear for his hearing, and so was automatically included on the list of people, most of them gangsters, who were banned from ever entering the state's casinos.

Although with his skills he could make a fortune on the endless satellite poker tournament that exists all over the country and on half the cruise ships at sea, he was done in Las Vegas. Now if he tried to have so much as a five-dollar buffet at a joint he could be arrested.

I had been around long enough to know mob associations meant nothing but trouble. They were like a skunk scent that never wore off. The legal gambling racket was built by the mob, but in the name of keeping up appearances and keeping out the federal government, the state got into the regulatory business. Today, licensees must pass background checks and receive privileged licenses, which are like solid gold permits to steal.

Ricky Billings had been just a kid, but now he looked as old as my knees felt.

"I saw you win the World Championship," I told him, without making eye contact. "You're quite a player."

"Was," he said. "I don't play cards anymore."

"That's lucky for the rest of us," I said. "Ever see any of the old crowd around?"

I had meant any of the real pros like Johnny Chan or Phil Hellmuth. But the kid was so obsessed he misunderstood me.

"Friends?" he asked. "Oh, yeah. They're behind me one hundred fifty percent. You must have read the papers. I've got the mob on my side. I'm on Easy Street. The fix is in. Follow me, and I'll give you a ride in my two-hundred-thousand-dollar, chauffeur-driven limousine with C-A-T written on the side. Friends? I never had any friends and I don't feel like making one."

"Not much chance of that, son," I said. "I just wanted to say I admired your skill, is all."

"My skill is what put me here on this bench, old-timer. I had so much skill I made a million dollars and never saw a dime of it. All I got was the headlines. That's how much skill I have."

There was nothing left to say. My knees were warm enough to make it the rest of the way around the lake. As I rose from the bench, the cormorants took flight.

It was then the former Ricky Billings tugged at my coat sleeve.

"In case anybody asks," he said, his old eyes looking into mine, "tell them I won that championship on the square."

Lucky Charm

As nothing is as it appears in Las Vegas, it stands to reason that the Midget's life would turn out to be bigger than his four-foot-two stature. He wasn't just the world's shortest bookmaker. He was a lucky charm, too.

I am not a big believer in rabbit feet and shiny pennies in shoes, but I try to respect the rituals of others. In Las Vegas, making fun of a man's system of luck is like ridiculing his religion. It's strictly poor form.

For years around the city the Midget was a living, breathing lucky charm. He'd been that way most of his life. At a time other boys were playing stickball on the streets of Brooklyn, the Midget was hustling newspapers and running errands for a dozen hoodlums, most notoriously the Gallo brothers. He was too small to park cars, but he hustled up sandwiches and turned up in the oddest places.

Yonkers Raceway one day, the Polo Grounds the next. He was everywhere, the Midget was, and so at an early age he gained a reputation as something of a talisman. When guys had big days at the track after seeing the Midget, they remembered him as the agent of change and rewarded him generously. Of course, when the round-heeled bum they bet a G-note on turned out to be a glass-jawed ham-and-egger, they took one look at the Midget and cursed their fates, then slipped him a few bucks to go stand near someone else. To them, he was either a walking four-leaf clover or a genuine Jonah.

Although he would have preferred to remain independent, for a while the Midget was on the edge of "Crazy Joe" Gallo's gang. Joe himself, those beady eyes burning anyone he gazed upon, believed the Midget brought good luck. By the time Crazy Joe's luck ran out one night inside Umberto's Clam House, the Midget had relocated to Las Vegas, where he toiled in obscurity for Jerry Zarowitz, one of the mob guys who fronted at Caesars Palace in those days.

He got into trouble with the sheriff and a few of his knee-crushing Task Force cops, but for the most part he managed to stay out of the spotlight. Not so Zarowitz, whose connections to the Genovese and Patriarca crime families were so well understood that even the Gaming Control Board caught up to him.

That development led the Midget to seek employment down the street at the Stardust, where he worked for Frank Rosenthal in the sports book next to its magicians, Marty Kane and Joey Boston.

Not that the Midget can be blamed for this, but within 18 months of his relocation Rosenthal was on his way out at the Stardust. Kane and Boston were axed, too. In fact, every mob family connected to the Teamsters' Central States Pension Fund was in trouble after the mob's casino skim operation was uncovered. Although the Midget was merely standing in the area, some guys, one of them being Joey Boston, had a feeling he'd brought the trouble with him.

After the Stardust, the Midget would show up at Caesars Palace in the morning, and bop from joint to joint telling anyone who'd listen his stories of old Las Vegas.

Anyone but Joey Boston, that is.

Joey believed to the depths of his shadowy soul that the Midget brought bad luck. Instantly. When Joey moved through the city, from Cafe Michelle to Piero's, he looked over his shoulder for the Midget as he sipped his Johnnie Walker. He'd pepper his sentences with references to the little guy, and how much he'd lost over the years whenever he appeared.

"It's like black magic or something," Joey would say.

Then he'd scoot off his barstool and head to the Sahara, where he played pan poker with a friend. One time while working a card game, I noticed Joey playing across the pit and waved to him. He called me over in a panic.

"Do me a favor and look around this joint for the Midget," he said. "Something's killing me here, and I swear it's got to be him. I can feel it."

I was skeptical but complied, then shrugged at him. No Midget. I made the sign of a drink, and he nodded. We'd meet up later at Cafe Michelle.

When I got there the bar was crowded except for one empty seat next to none other than the little man Joey hated so much. I asked the Midget what was new.

"Bad things, I'm afraid," he said. "It seems our friend Joey Boston suffered a massive heart attack at one of the clubs today. They revived him after a few minutes, but there's little hope."

I was upset, but tried to make small talk. Then he said something that made me rethink my Las Vegas belief system.

I told him, "I was at the Sahara earlier today, and talked to Joey."

"What a coincidence," the Midget said. "I was there, too."

Tip Money

When I had money, I was always George with the help. Ask anybody who knew me then. Even when I blew plenty on the pros or colleges, or a big fight, I always kept enough in reserve for the people I met.

I set no records, but I think a five-dollar bill is a healthy toke for a cup of coffee. For dinner, I might drop fifty or a hundred if the service was nice and depending on who was watching. Because I'm like a lot of guys who believe success breeds success, I'd sprinkle the cabbage patch with greenbacks. Scared money never amounts to anything, and so I've never worried too much about any amount that would fit in my front pocket.

But tip money matters. Believe it. At a downtown coffee shop one morning, I ordered black coffee and rye toast, read my newspapers. That was my daily routine. After digesting the news, I'd get a more substantial breakfast.

That's the day I met Tina the Ballerina, who wasn't small at all but short and squatty. She had a tired but kind face that only a few years and forty pounds earlier had been pretty. She moved with the grace of a dancer. A jazz dancer, not the exotic kind.

The first few times she waited on me, she greeted me warmly. I ordered quietly, tipped generously, and went about my business. I guess she'd waited on me once a week for three months when she interrupted my newspaper reading by spilling a coffee refill over the front page of the Times.

"Oh, my God, I'm so sorry," she said, wiping furiously. "You've been so nice and I repay you by ruining your morning."

Her plump face was blushing.

"Nothing lost," I said. "The news will be just as bad tomorrow."

"Please accept my apologies." she gushed. "I'm so sorry, Mr. ...?"

"Crabbe, Jasper Crabbe," I said.

"I apologize, Jasper," she said. Her eyes were surprisingly blue. They were the eyes that belonged to a beautiful woman.

I calmed her down, and she went away, only to return a few minutes later with a fresh newspaper. The act of kindness impressed me.

She bought breakfast, but I had money in those days and simply added the price of the check onto her tip, which brought the meal to about twenty-five dollars.

I rose to leave and expected her to bid me farewell, but Tina was nowhere near. Probably in the kitchen, I thought, leaving the counter and crossing through the casino. By the time I got outside, I glanced to my left and saw her standing next to me without her apron and hat. Her uniform was dark and made of polyester, but it held her in one place. She was a handsome woman, round and pleasant, although certainly not my type. My

sort of woman ran toward the tall and chronically alcoholic. She was short and merely exhausted by life. I was
at least twice her age.

"I just wanted to apologize again to you," she said, walking with me in the direction of the Union Plaza.

"That's nice of you, but it really isn't necessary," I replied.

"You've been awfully nice to me these past few months.
Most people don't realize it, but the tips really make a
big difference for me."

"I understand," I said.

"I'm sure you do," she said. "I know you've probably
seen enough of me for one day, but you wouldn't happen
to be driving toward Flamingo and the Strip, would you?
I need a ride home and my car's in the shop."

"All right."

We rode in silence south on Las Vegas Boulevard.
Traffic was light, and in a few minutes she had directed
me to her apartment behind the Imperial Palace. I'd been
through the area many times. It was where many Las
Vegas immigrants started out or ended up.

She directed me to a parking space outside a shabby
fourplex.

"Please, won't you come in for a cup of coffee?" she
said, placing her slightly greasy little hand on mine. "My
children are with the neighbors until noon, and I'd like
to make you a good cup of coffee."

The way she squeezed my hand told me she'd be serving something else.

Now I know what you're probably thinking. She wasn't
my type. She probably wasn't anybody's type. She wasn't

a handsome woman by many definitions. Nor was she the brightest bulb in the intellectual marquee.

But there was something in the air, perhaps the smell of ham and eggs on her uniform, perhaps the hint of longing in her pale blue eyes, that made me accept her offer.

Some people need to be needed, others need to be wanted. Occasionally, one stranger just wants to show another a little gratitude. These days, I take my gratitude where I find it.

What is life, after all, without an occasional cup of coffee?

SEX AND VIOLINS

You need not be hit over the head with an oboe to notice that Las Vegas is not a world center for classical music.

There is a local symphony these days, and the university graduates a few aspiring Beethovens, but for the most part the town was built on Muzak and mainsteam jazz, the kind veteran players pounded out night after night in a backup capacity for Capitol crooners and hyperbolic saloon singers.

Las Vegas has sometimes aspired to the highbrow, but has always been more comfortable with the bump and grind. A civilized man would find it far easier to locate a tastefully decorated strip joint than the next meeting of the Mozart society.

For my part, I keep tuned to National Public Radio, which plays classical music, opera standards and liberal news. Although I am not formally educated, and my ear is somewhat tinny after an accident involving an explosion some years ago, I have managed to learn to distinguish Mozart from Mendelsohn, *La Boheme* from *The Barber of Seville.*

The idea of culture impresses the masses and especially the newly rich inside the casino business. Guys whose pedigrees go back not to the Metropolitan Opera but to Murder Inc. start using the king's English when Art, Literature and Classical Music are discussed. Their opinions are always insightful. And they are never wrong and blessed with uncommon taste. Just ask any of the lackeys who work for them.

Looking back, I'm sure that's what attracted Harry Schiller to Las Vegas. I met Harry at my office, which in those days was located at the Philly Pub. I was moving a little money and having a good spring when this distinguished-looking gentleman took a seat at the bar next to me and ordered a brandy. He had a shock of white hair that had been cut that day, a hawk's nose and the beady eyes of a bird of prey. He was not handsome, but distinctive. His suit was tailored, not quite Italian but something close. He wore an expensive silk tie into a shot-and-a-beer joint. He also wore a cologne that pierced the cigarette smoke and smelled almost tropical. Imperious, proper. Well-heeled and wealthy, with a hint of mystery. That was the image Harry Schiller projected.

Beyond the incongruity of discovering a dandy amid the construction workers, nurses and insurance salesmen, I thought nothing of the man.

He was too square to be a pimp, too conservatively dressed for a pit boss. As the Philly was located near a county hospital and a funeral parlor, a coincidence I always found a bit unnerving, the stranger could have been coming from some devastatingly emotional experience such as the bedside of a gravely ill loved one or the gateway to the graveyard.

As I hate boorish chatter in bars, I respected his space and privacy, but my curiosity got the better of me when I saw him glance at his watch. It was almost a Rolex. I say almost because he let it hang in the light long enough for a trained eye to observe that its style was Swiss and expensive but its glint was all wrong. Nice try, though.

It occurred to me the old bird might be working me, but unless Metro or the FBI had slipped a new face into their organized crime/bookmaking detail, the stranger was no member of law enforcement. I sipped my drink, sized him up, then blurted out, "Jasper Crabbe. Commodities."

"Mr. Commodities. Fascinating name," he said in a dry, proper British accent. "Schiller, Harold Schiller. World Philharmonic and BBC Orchestra, semi-retired."

"A pleasure to meet you," I said. "I've been waiting years for the class of clientele to improve."

"Yes, quite," he said. "Any port in a storm, I suppose."

I bought Harold Schiller a drink and welcomed him to the Philly Pub. For the next 20 minutes we discussed the state of classical music and its potential in Southern Nevada. He dropped several names, and along the way mentioned that although he had conducted orchestras for much of his life, his real love was the violin, which he had played as a guest soloist before the greatest orchestras of Europe and the Boston Pops, Cleveland Symphony and others.

After he finished his drink, he said, "You look like a man who appreciates the finer things. I've run into the strangest luck, something that could only occur in your Las Vegas, I suppose. But I recently performed for a group of Saudi high-rollers at a private casino function. They enjoyed the program, of course, and even though my bow hand's gone arthritic I was in fine fiddle, pun intended. Trouble is, when it came time to go they wanted to be gracious and so one of the gentlemen gave me his watch. It's a splendid piece, but I'm afraid I already have one that I'm particularly fond of."

With that, he showed me his left and right wrists. Both appeared to have identical watches. The difference was, the one on his right wrist was duller, and if I had to bet, I'd guess it was authentic. He slipped it off and showed it to me. I was right. He chatted a few more minutes, said he was told it was worth ten-thousand dollars, but since he'd bought his for twenty five hundred years ago he wouldn't dream of accepting more than that. Wouldn't be fair, Harold Schiller of the World Philharmonic and BBC Orchestra said.

"Too rich for me, I'm afraid," I said, wanting to see where he was going with his patter. "There's a group of doctors that comes in after five on Thursdays. They might be interested."

"Pardon me, then," he said. "When you said commodities, naturally I thought—"

"That I had a few bucks to spend. Perfectly understandable. No offense taken."

With that, he checked his watches.

"Right, then, I must be off," Harold Schiller said, thrusting a hand to shake. I returned it. Our eyes smiled, each knowing the lies that had just transpired. With that, he left the bar.

I finished my drink and decided to move up the street. I'd been holding too much cash and ran the risk of being robbed. I hate holding too much cash. Leaving the parking lot, I glanced across Charleston Boulevard toward the bus stop. There, standing with four ordinary working stiffs, was the perfectly proper figure of Harold Schiller, waiting for the crosstown bus.

• • •

The next time I saw Harry Schiller, three months had passed. But he was not hard to spot. He wore an expensive tux, diamond cufflinks and no doubt a genuine Rolex as he stood with the posture of a European prince beneath the portico of the Dunes Hotel. The bright lights of the entrance highlighted his white hair and made his profile look all the more regal.

Some guys know how to stand so it appears they are in the center of everything important and the rest of the world flows around them. Harry knew how to stand.

The aging matron on his arm saw nothing more than his hawk's profile, of that I am certain. Her gaze was bunny-eyed and glassy, and she laughed giddily at his shared observation as they waited for the valet to bring around their car. Given the fact the last time I'd seen Harry he was standing at a bus stop, I couldn't wait to see what model of automobile he was riding in.

Because they were focused on valet and each other, I was able to stand within two feet of them under the crowded colonnade without being recognized. I was close enough to hear fragments of their conversation.

"Rachmaninoff was a bloody bastard to deal with," he said with his convincing, if overstated, British accent. "Brilliant, of course, but a bastard nonetheless. Of course, his English was dreadful, and my Russian a bit rusty, so perhaps it was the language barrier."

His starry-eyed date giggled.

Harry winked knowingly. She squeezed his arm.

"But there's one thing old Sergei showed me, and that is that no community is ever truly civilized without developing an educated affection for music," he said. "Las Vegas is really a marvelous place in its way, but, well, let's just say it's no Vienna, if you know what I mean."

Apparently she did, for she nodded like a schoolgirl and kept her eyes locked on his.

"I don't suppose there's anything to be done but sit back and enjoy another lounge crooner, or pray for some small ensemble to be created," he said. "But you know, Margie, my love, I dream of greater things for us. I have been a resident only a few short weeks, but I see its potential for greatness. It has an electricity about it that's palpable. It has the raw ingredients of a world-class city, a place apart from the madding crowd, something more than a gambling mecca, more than a place for all these bloody tourists. No, my dear, I dream of greater things for this diamond in the rough, things, I dare say, that you and I might accomplish together."

"I would like that very much, Harold," she said, dreamily.

"Really, Margie, my love, call me Harry," he said. "I prefer it. Harold is the renowned violinist, composer and conductor. Harry is your fast friend and, if I may be so bold, your unabashedly admiring suitor, one who basks in your beauty and prays you will see him again."

"Oh, Harry, you're so sweet," she said, blushing in the neon light. "I'd love to see you again."

"Music to my trained ears," Harry replied.

Both laughed knowingly. He patted her hand.

Harry drew a breath and kept up his patter.

"It was something Gershwin, whom I knew well, recognized about America," he said. "America was possessed of many things, not least of which its indefatigable spirit and sense of creativity, but save jazz it lacked a truly classical statement. There were fine performers, conductors and composers. I must tell you some time about my tiff with Samuel Barber not long after he wrote *Adagio for Strings*. But Gershwin knew that only a classically based music would raise America to the highest heights on the world stage. And so he pursued a career that, as you know, attempted to weave the great American jazz spirit with a sense of the classical aesthetic. Witness his efforts on *Rhapsody in Blue, An American in Paris.* Clearly American classical music, not traditional long-haired but smashing nonetheless, don't you think? You would have liked old George, who was quite a wit, I must say."

Just then her Mercedes pulled up to the curb. He escorted her to the passenger-side door, and the valet handed him the keys.

As they pulled away, I noticed the license plate read, "Burke."

"So that was Fast Eddie Burke's billion-dollar widow," I thought.

They made a handsome couple.

•••

The last time I saw Harry Schiller, he was being interviewed on television while standing next to a beaming Margie Burke, Outfit casino man Eddie Burke's very rich widow. It was classic local TV news drivel, and Harry filled every second of airtime with his authoritative British accent and big talk of a classical music conservatory that would finally give Las Vegas the status it so richly deserved. Margie Burke, generous lady that she was, had consented to donate the first one million toward land acquisition and construction, and several of her friends had agreed in principal to make substantial donations. The school would be known as the Burke-Schiller Center for Classical Studies, Harold Schiller Director.

My man had come a long way from the afternoon in the Philly Pub, but I had to wonder whether he knew what he was getting into with anyone related to Eddie Burke. Eddie was easily one of the most powerful men in Las Vegas while alive, and I'd place him in the top ten even a decade after his death. Once connected, always connected.

I made sure to pick up copies of the papers the next day to read the puff pieces on Harold Schiller and his benefactress, Margaret Burke, university donor and widow of the late casino man. No mention in the stories that Schiller was a con artist straight from the street. And heaven forbid there be even a paragraph on the fact that Fast Eddie had made his fortune not in the casino business, but in running prostitutes in Cicero for Al Capone before moving out to Las Vegas ahead of the law. Like Harold Schiller, Eddie had reinvented himself as a friend of stray pets and orphans. Burke was a pimp and a killer elsewhere, but in Las Vegas he was a good Joe who over-tipped the Sunday collection plate and bought his way into the pantheon of local legends right next to Benny Binion and Moe Dalitz. Somewhere along the way he'd bought a free pass from Hank Greenspun and Don Reynolds, the owners of the local newspapers, who must have liked him for his ebullient personality and not because he was capable of advertising his casino and other holdings in their rags to the tune of half a mill a year. Yeah, it was charity all around in Las Vegas.

So maybe Margie Burke was getting what she deserved and Harry Schiller, or whatever his name was, was going to have the last laugh and finally make a big score. I couldn't blame a scuffler for dreaming big. Who was I but another mope on the street working for peanuts and a few track tips?

A few weeks went by and I got busy with the start of the football season. Like most other professional players and all those who believe they are, I spend hours poring over statistics hoping to glean a sense from the chaotic maze. The worst thing a player can do is to believe the numbers add up to something approaching a higher sci-ence. Truth is, the games are still games and anything can happen. What the smart player tries to do is develop the quality of his opinions on teams, players, coaches. That developed sense works outside the sports book, too.

It's always a busy time of year for a runner. And so I stopped thinking so much about the Burke-Schiller Center for Classical Studies, Harold Schiller Director. In the back of my mind, though, the numbers were tumbling. If he pulled it off, Harry was a genius.

But if he was a genius, what was he doing at the Philly Pub that day?

I handicapped the situation, placed my over-under on Schiller's life expectancy at nine months. For a while I thought I'd missed something when I read of their engagement in one of the society columns. Around New Year's, I heard they'd gotten married at the top of the Dunes.

I've lost plenty of bets in my life, so I wasn't devastated to learn the following spring that the ground was broken on the Burke-Schiller Center. It looked like maybe I had been wrong about them as a couple. Perhaps I was even wrong about Harry Schiller. Could that fake Rolex have been real?

May 1, 1979. I picked up the paper.

"Musician Found Dead," the headline read.

Former Strip violinist Arthur C. Martin, sixty-seven, who was also known as Harold Schiller, had been found shot to death in the desert less than a mile from the Dunes. He wasn't from England. He was from Scranton. Story said plans for the Burke-Schiller Center were on hold.

Police named robbery as the apparent motive. That didn't exactly explain why someone had broken his hands and shot him through the heart, but then this was Las Vegas.

Next time I went back to the Philly Pub I gave a silent toast to Harry Schiller and reminded myself not to date out of my weight class.

Yangtze Moon

was downtown and busted again, angling toward Fifth
and Fremont and working on a pretty good drunk when
it happened. My epiphany, my haiku butterfly floating
down from the cold night.

Not actually floating, buzzing like an angry hornet
was more like it.

I had spent the better part of Friday working a couple
of low-stakes hold'em games at Binion's and had run into
a chainsaw of bad beats. After two hours I was like the
knight in the Monty Python movie. No arms, no legs,
blood flowing everywhere, but still popping off.

I picked up while I still had walking-around money
and moved to the Four Queens, where I have become
acquainted with the afternoon blackjack crew. I do the
aw-shucks routine with them, and they let me count their
cards as long as I remember to toke the help, which I
always do. This routine usually flattens out my bad luck
and sends me on my way with cash in pocket for the
coming week.

But not this Friday. On this Friday I lose six straight
hands, get a gift from the dealer and then drop five more.
Win two, lose ten. Win one, lose nine.

Out of the corner of my eye, I can see Rod Serling
with his arms crossed, smoking and asking strangers to

consider the plight of Jasper Crabbe as he spirals ever deeper into *The Twilight Zone.*

Inside of an hour I can feel the imprint of the remaining change in my pocket pressing against my leg. For sucker sport I win two straight bets and think I am returning to form, then drop two. Right now I can't count to twenty-one.

I understand the mathematical percentages of a gambler's luck. It's only gambling for the player. For the house, it's just renting space. The house over time is far luckier than the player, but this was something beyond that. It was karma or black magic, or maybe a sign.

I emerged with a fistful of free drink coupons, a comped buffet and maybe nine bucks in folding money, plus a pocketful of pay phone change. Nice day's work if you're a fun book Freddy.

Which I guess I was becoming, slowly but surely. And so I plunked down four drink tickets and ordered tequila shots for all my partners. Since they don't drink, I felt compelled to consume them myself.

My tequila head is different from my everyday head, and substantially different from my ordinary booze head. With my tequila head, I am more inclined to recite the work of my old friend Li Po, who died in 762 but sings to me still with his brilliant, boozy sing-songy voice.

"I take my wine jug out among the flowers," I blurted to a group of tourists, whose tragic-comic faces told me I was really out of line this time. "I drink alone, without friends, and raise my cup to entice the moon. That, and my shadow, makes us three."

By this time I am not only drinking alone, but walking alone as well. The people I meet are all coming the other way, up Fremont toward the heart of the Experience, which I recommend you visit only after bolting on your tequila head. I duck in at the Atomic and contribute all my change and a couple of greenbacks besides and make five ounces of Montezuma clear disappear like gasoline in an old tank.

I'm downtown, where all the lights are bright, looking for the Yangtze moon Li Po fell in love with, when my tequila head notices trouble. These are not the lights of the Fremont Street Experience, but the flashing red and blue lights of six Metro patrol cars blocking the lower end of the street and preventing me from mingling amid the motel district and, since I have just seven dollars in my pocket, a prostitute with a familiar face, a sense of humor and willingness to play on credit.

The police haven't thrown up a line yet, but the bystanders are moving away as I stumble toward the action.

Suddenly, my epiphany.

A shot rings out, then what sounds like fifty more. I stand there twenty feet from a standoff that ends with one rotund Mexican man in his underwear catching enough lead to turn his T-shirt crimson.

One of the bullets ricochets and ka-thwongs by my ear so close I can feel the breeze of the hornet's wings. I am stunned, suddenly sober, thousands of memories coursing through my brain.

Luck is relative.

My addled mind settles on a line from one of Li Po's distant students, who wrote, "Even a street dog has his lucky days."

I am that street dog. My laughter howls like a madman reborn, and I shuffle off toward home as the full moon rises over Fremont Street.

PART II: NEON CHEESE

Ted's Perfect Day

Ted was as straight as he'd been in months. The juvenile court mediator had told him to check the calendar and wise up, that he wouldn't be able to act a fool much longer before he'd no longer qualify for the kiddie treatment. Ted had tried to take the guy seriously, but he was such a Gomer. It was like, nice crewcut, Sgt. Carter, now get out of my face.

Besides, this time the rent-a-judge was wrong. Ted hadn't eaten a hit of speed in weeks and no longer drank beer, even on the weekends. So he needed the lecture from the dork with the flat top like he needed another year of high school.

Problem with being chemical-free was, he'd fallen asleep again in class, and to the teachers who knew his reputation as a stoner that meant only one thing: drug nod. It wasn't true, and he'd told them they were out of their minds, only more colorfully. That had drawn the attention of the campus police, who were on a full-name basis with Theodore Roosevelt Leen. While the bruising teacher and a nebbish administrator traded notes, Ted could tell by the tone of their voices that they thought he was a hopeless loser and a waste of their vast educational acumen. The cops had cuffed him, which the other kids thought was pretty cool, but Ted believed was excessive and violated his rights. Not that anyone cared. Plenty of his fellow students figured he'd better get used to the feel of handcuffs.

Besides the lecture and the weekend in juvee before his grandma could pick him up, he was basically free to go about his business. He occasionally attended Western High as a junior and was told by his teachers that they knew he was smart enough to do the work, but he just didn't care enough to succeed. Whatever. It wasn't like anyone he knew actually used algebra or had heard of anyone who'd ever used algebra, so what did he care if he ever learned the difference between a quadratic equation and a queen of hearts? School to him was all like some quiz show that ran day after day. A few of the contestants get all the cash and prizes and glory while the rest received lovely parting gifts and lifetime supplies of Rice-A-Roni.

He couldn't see where it mattered all that much if he got an A in English or a C as long as his teacher left him alone to sleep in the back of the class. English was his first period of the day and he was always nodding off. The other students believed he was just another freak, one of the legion of long hairs who wore scraggy chin whiskers, Army jackets and combat boots or busted-out sneakers. Stoners smoked like the blue-hairs who play the nickel slots at the El Cortez and are always on the scrounge for a pack of butts or a pinch of primo. Ted didn't bother to tell them he worked until six a.m. as a busboy at the Casa Grande Casino on Sixth and Fremont, pulling egg-stained plates off tables, emptying ashtrays and refilling coffee cups for the bums, burnouts and crack whores, some of whom were sitting when he arrived at nine-thirty and still there when he left at six.

Ted's eyes felt like they'd been sanded by an entire woodshop class, and his mouth reeked of too much bad coffee. He drank two and sometimes three pots just to stay awake. It made his heart jackhammer and gave him the shakes and the runs, but it kept him from falling asleep in the middle of his shift. The middle of graveyard was always hardest, like the midpoint of a marathon from hell. You hit the wall and it seems like nothing you do will keep you from curling up in a booth and letting sleep hit you in the head like a cartoon anvil. Coffee got him through, even if his ears rang and he hallucinated a bit.

The job was not without its perks. Drug dealers occasionally tipped him a little dope, and he'd had sex with one of the waitresses, a squat but surprisingly energetic matron with billowing breasts and too much makeup. He'd been propositioned a few times by the street girls and once by a heroin-junkie-slim ass hustler named Rusty. But even now when he thought about it, it scared him to know he couldn't see himself reflected in their dead eyes.

The casino cafe job wasn't how he pictured himself. It was just something he did to earn money to help his grandmother pay the bills.

His shift made it almost impossible for him to concentrate in school. He tried to keep up without letting on that he cared too much. He always managed to turn in his composition papers even if he had to write them in the pantry of the kitchen during his breaks. He turned in one on a big sheet of butcher paper once and managed to pull off a D. Math wasn't hard since he'd given up trying to advance, and the rest was a bunch of babble of warmed-over history and lightweight current events. Ted read the newspapers and paperback novels customers left behind and knew enough about the Middle East and the federal budget to fake his way through World History and Government. He could imitate Mickey Spillane and had read Portnoy's Complaint three times, and not just for the kink. It had been his observation that adults spent most of their time faking their way through life.

Although he'd never admit it, the truth was he was glad to be back in school. He hated the busboy job and itched for something more. Being in class felt safe even if he wasn't a good student. He'd seen enough to know there were worse things than being bored by Chaucer and writing essays titled "My Perfect Day."

On the morning he decided to graduate, he came straight from work to school early. He napped in the morning sun on the grass next to the baseball field, felt the warmth of new daylight on his face, and listened to the distant sounds of sparrows and students arriving. The air was cool and sweet and he felt so light he thought he might levitate by sheer will. At that moment, he would have sworn he was invisible, as if he were part of the Earth itself.

He realized he belonged in school and not running the street and working a dead-end Vegas job. He knew his next move would have been to learn to deal, and by then it might be too late. As much as he hated to admit it, school was the only way out.

Although he did not know religion, Ted had an epiphany and awoke with his eyes wet with tears.

Rested, he washed up in the P.E. locker room, got to class before the bell, and insisted on raising his hand and answering two questions. He knew people were watching him, waiting for him to fail.

On that perfect spring morning, he decided to make them wait a long, long time.

SCARY MARY

I have to laugh every time I pass her billboard or one of her hundreds of handsome yard signs. "One Call, No Job Too Big Or Small. Mary _____ Realty."

Her face has changed in twenty years. She has a new nose and smoother skin. She's no longer a bleach bottle blonde, and the hard-living crow's feet have been surgically stretched. She's even had those vampire teeth of hers fixed.

But she's still my Scary Mary. Well, not exactly mine. Everybody's, is more like it.

Before she rivaled the bald personal injury attorney for face time on billboards across the valley, Mary was known to the construction payday party crowd as Scary Mary. Scary for a couple of reasons. First her teeth had been chipped and resembled fangs, the sort Bela Lugosi flashed in Dracula movies. Only Mary's appeared whenever she opened her mouth, which was often at working-class bars during the mid-1980s building boom.

Beyond her dental defects, Mary was not a handsome woman, not even by bad bar light. Plain and not skinny. Almost flat-chested with a manliness to her shoulders that would remind some customers of a journeyman bricklayer.

She had a knack for finding the backstreet bars where the tapers, ironworkers and cement finishers went to cash and spend their paychecks on Friday afternoon. While they were blowing their wages, she made a fortune blowing them. The woman inspected more groins than a dozen Army physicians. She was one of the most prolific sword-swallowers this circus has ever seen.

She'd set up shop in the women's room, which was rarely used in those construction bars. She'd pay off the bartender in cash or trade, and start working when the first of the hardhat crews busted through the door. She waited until the paychecks were cashed and the bills were fat in their front pockets, then set to work.

Her first few propositions were so brazen they were often met with incredulous looks, but a shrug from the bartender told the workers her offer was honorable and not some sick police sting. Is there any easier and more cruel law enforcement joke than propositioning men for sex?

It's like asking a dog if he'd like a bone. For that matter, the community's sex laws are the height of hypocrisy, but that's an issue for another day.

Scary Mary worked harder than a Mexican roofer. She probably could have charged twice what she received, which was ten dollars, but she more than made up in volume. Not to mention the tips.

And to my knowledge she never went further than the oral end of the business. At least not in a bar packed with a hundred sweaty construction hacks. Men sometimes offered her half their checks to accompany them to a more comfortable setting than the urine-stained stall she used, but Mary never went. She was a one-trick pony who never seemed to tire of the same old thing.

She sometimes dumped the cash in her trunk. On especially busy nights, she went to the trunk two or three times in a night after making her rounds. And she only worked paydays, as far as I know. The rest of the week she went to school and studied for the real estate exam.

About the time the last of the customers emerged grinning and zipping from the ladies room, Mary would emerge with fresh makeup and a purse jammed full of cash and her black .38 snubby—often to cheers from the entire bar. All the world's a stage, right?

In the years I saw her around town in her previous life, the only time she ever made the newspaper was when a particularly foolish customer got out of line and lost one of his testicles in what police described as a lover's quarrel that got out of hand.

Her gun once belonged to a police officer, a man she married and divorced. I met him once. He was crying in his vodka at the Rice Paddy, lamenting the loss of his one true love. Perhaps I knew her, he said. Her name was Mary _____, the realtor with all the signs. He was miserable because he saw her face wherever he went.

"Know her?" I said. "Sure, I know her. Not well, but everybody knows Mary. 'One call, no job too big or small.'"

The drunk cop nodded, muttered something about her running off with some hot-shot congressional candidate. He didn't catch the name.

Good Customers

That Rosa had been a good kid, a Mexican, but a good kid, Bev thought. She was a hustler, you had to give her that.

She always kept the tables around her station wiped down and set up and never got cow eyes at the end of the shift when Bev toked her a few singles after a very good night. Most bus help is either young and irresponsible, drunk and irresponsible, or old and ornery. A few, and she had to admit that most of them were the Mexicans or the Vietnamese, actually treated the job like they were grateful to have one. That Rosa always seemed happy to get whatever share of the night's tokes Bev bestowed upon her. Grateful, clean and subservient—just the way Bev liked it.

Especially when the good customers came in.

Bev had been around since Gus Greenbaum's time and knew the score. The two young men dressed in baggy plaid shirts and droopy blue jeans might have looked like a couple of cartoon bums, but they were high-rollers around the casino. The styles had changed, but Bev knew when players were in action, and these two were in action.

They dominated booth number three on the edge of Bev's station and arrived each night at two. Bev knew the score. Their beepers went off like racetrack trumpets every few minutes or so, and one or the other would get up from the booth and go to the Buckaroo Bar to meet a friend. Occasionally, one would get a phone call and excuse himself to go to the men's room or out to the lobby or parking lot.

Never gone more than a few minutes, always in the booth a couple or three hours. Like clockwork. When they got up after meals of steak and eggs and orange juice, a couple beers shots of tequila, they always left twenty dollars apiece.

Bev had worked showrooms in the '60s when a double sawbuck was no big deal and wouldn't buy you more than the handshake it came with, but it was a long way from the Stardust to the Ranch House Casino, and a forty-dollar tip was nothing to sniff at. So she found herself looking for them each night and greeting them like high-rollers when they entered the mouth of the cafe. She waved them over with a smile and the sweep of an arm and snarled whenever another waitress tried to get friendly.

"Good evening, gentlemen," she'd say. "I held your regular booth for you."

Unless they were ready to order, they rarely spoke to Bev, only nodded with sleepy eyes and slid into the booth, where they spoke in whispers and nods. When she overheard them, they spoke Spanish with English jammed in.

The last time she saw the pair was on a night they'd been busier than usual, making several trips each from the table. At one point, the table was empty for fifteen minutes, the plates of steaks and eggs left untouched.

Bev got busy with other customers for a few minutes and lost track of booth No. 3. When she turned around, her good customers were standing at the table staring at Rosa, who cowered in their presence. Rosa had cleared their dishes, removed their cups and glasses and wiped down the table. The two men were not amused, and Bev could feel them slipping away.

She rushed over.

"What seems to be the matter?"

Rosa said, "I think they are gone. I cleared the table. I'm very sorry."

"You little idiot. These gentlemen weren't finished. They were busy, and now they're hungry. Get out of my sight or I'll have your job."

"I'm very sorry," Rosa said, tears rolling down her cheeks.

"Gentlemen," Bev said, "I'll be happy to place your order again. I'll get the cook on it right away. I'll see to it personally, and of course will pick up your check."

Her good customers merely grunted, conversed briefly in Spanish, and left the cafe. Rosa turned in her badge and did not return for her final paycheck.

Bev went back to her station. For the next few weeks, she found herself looking for the two men each night around their usual time. She never saw her high-rollers or that bus girl again.

"Stupid Mexicans," Bev mumbled to herself. "The whole town's gone to hell."

MEMORIES AND PIGEONS

Simon sat on the bench in Huntridge Park with a shopping bag at his side, two-dozen pigeons at his feet, and suddenly, a quarter-sized white spot on his shoe. He saw the spot and laughed. The birds did not stir.

"Oh, Barney, always the creative wit," Simon said, removing two slices of dry white bread from the bag. He broke the slices and spread them among the birds. "My, that was a good one."

All gray and black, brown and white and even red, the pigeons strutted and pecked before him like a cooing congregation. Simon adjusted his old coat and hat and coughed to clear his throat.

"If you aren't the busiest bunch today," he said, reaching for more feed, courtesy of the dumpster located behind the ReadyMart downtown. "And where to now, Mr. and Mrs. White? Off to the halls of justice for the evening? And Prince Charles and Lady Diana, perhaps you will take in the new Renoir exhibit at the gallery; I so love the Impressionists. I know you'll take your entourage. And of course I know where you, one-legged Mike, and you, Barney of the unabashed bowels, and the rest of you boys are headed: It's the ballgame and a few beers downtown."

In the filtered spring light touching the bench, Simon looked almost young, perhaps no more than sixty, instead of eighty-two. In that light, the birds moved as silhouettes, bobbing ghosts flown in from the past. One bird fluttered up from the sidewalk to the bench next to Simon.

"And you, my dear, sweet Clara girl, where will we fly tonight? To the river, perhaps, to feel the cool air? To the heart of Fremont to take in the lights and commotion and tastes the snacks of the street? Or maybe, my love, we'll fly to a distant church steeple and coo all night long."

Simon eased back on the bench, coughed a little, and closed his eyes in the late afternoon shadows. Lulled by the cooing, he began to doze and saw his sweet Clara in her wedding dress, with the children, and as the bright beauty he had loved for sixty-five years. As Simon slipped further into sleep, a blond boy on a fast bicycle came screaming up the sidewalk. Wheels whizzing, chain rattling, the bicycle parted the pigeons like a feathered puddle, waking the old man and stunning one gray bird. Simon straightened himself on the bench and watched the boy on the bicycle recede from view. Then he saw the injured bird.

"You're not well, Barney boy, not well at all," he said, gathering up the pigeon. "Rest awhile."

He cradled the bird and it began to regain its addled senses. Barney wanted to curse the teenager, but instead found himself thinking of the boy's hair and how his own hair had once been as blond as corn silk.

In a few moments, the bird flapped and dropped a teaspoon of white soup in Simon's hands. The old man laughed as the pigeon flew away and rejoined his mates.

"Oh, Barney," Simon said. "That's a good one."

• • •

The dream was always the same, Simon searching relentlessly through the hairy dark for his lost angel. Through ankle-deep muck, over barren hills, his legs ached in the dream. He walked until he came to a ridge beyond which only cool air flowed. A pit, but nothing so ominous as a pit.

He stood on the edge and listened and tried to see through the darkness. Gradually, as if arriving in slow flight, he heard the pigeons cooing, then the easy whoosh of wings, then the breathing of his sweet Clara. He stood in the darkness and spoke to her without sound. Their meeting was like a scene from a silent movie. They laughed about town dances and country socials more than a half century old.

He stood on the edge and smiled as the light, sunlight perhaps, it was as gradual as sunlight, seeped into the dark chasm. He wanted to step forward and meet the light, but could not. He heard doves cooing, or perhaps pigeons. Pigeons are doves, too, Simon told himself in the dream. Every night he trekked through mire, across warm, humid land only to reach the edge of the great empty space without taking the final step. It wasn't courage he lacked, exactly, it was timing. The moment was not right. In time, he hoped, in time.

Simon awoke with perspiration on his brow. A frustration bear-hugged his heart and made his breathing difficult. Another long night's journey into day, he thought. As the swamp cooler kicked on, he smelled her again. That half-lilac, half-woman scent had never left the old place. It lasted only a moment in the early morning. It was as if Clara had only just left the room.

In the bathroom, he attempted to pee but failed. In the kitchen, he thought of having a big breakfast to cheer himself, but couldn't eat more than toast. He liked toast more and more. With just a little butter and no jam. Yes, he liked toast. And tea, not coffee. Coffee upset his system, made him go involuntarily. One minute it would make him deathly constipated, the next he would be going like a goose across the grass. But toast, lightly buttered, was just fine.

Simon heated water, had his toast and tea and waited for "As the World Turns" to come on the television. He liked soap operas, though he would never admit it in company. He watched his program, but got no satisfaction from it. It was Clara, always Clara.

He walked toward the ReadyMart and thought of the time they had saved their money and bought tickets to the San Francisco Ballet and how they cried at the beauty of the delicate dancers. And there was the time, in the early years, when they would go dancing to beat the band at the El Rancho on Saturday night, and eat at the Chinaman's afterward. So many memories, Simon thought, reaching into the dumpster and removing several loaves of stale bread. But when all a man has left are memories, it's not a good thing. Memories and pigeons, memories and pigeons.

Simon waited some time on his bench at Huntridge Park, and the afternoon was stretching like a cat, and the pigeons still had not arrived. The punks with their terrible broom straw haircuts and music like jackhammers came and went. The Mexican boys with their hotrods that almost scraped the ground cruised by, too.

"Running about the town all day, errands and luncheons and socials," Simon said, breaking up the bread and preparing the meal. "Errands and luncheons and socials."

The old man leaned back to get a good view of the horizon above the housetops and below the elm branches, and in a while he saw the dark specks in the distant blue. As they grew, he perked up and began spreading some of the bread. Tired, perhaps from his poor night's sleep, he yawned as the first of the birds touched the earth near his feet.

"Hello, boy. Good to see you back again. How was the ballgame? And how many beers did you drink? Boys, you know what that'll get you. I see you, Barney, are none the worse for wear, you old coot."

The other birds lit around him on the grass, and their flapping wings cooled his perspiration as he stretched out on the bench. He dropped the bread and leaned back too fast.

The muck did not slow him this time, and the hills were no match for his strong legs. He pressed on, carrying with him his secret like a Christmas kitten in his coat pocket. Already he heard the cooing, already he felt and saw the glow in the distance. And suddenly, there he was, on the edge and waiting as the frustration melted away by the moment. He smiled as he saw her, and he hopped forward and felt the world fall away.

From treetop level, the old man appeared to be sleeping on the bench as old men will do in the late afternoon. As the Huntridge Park pigeons flapped and swirled into the afternoon sky, the pigeon man and his angel Clara were testing fresh wings and cooing to beat the band.

Price of Gold

was walking down First toward Fremont in front of a certain pawnshop, contemplating America's infatuation with sports figures, when out of nowhere a jolt to the left shoulder spun me like an autumn leaf.

"Sorry, buddy," a foggy baritone said.

When my eyes focused, I found myself face to scarred face with none other than Buddy "Bump" Boyer, the former cruiserweight champion of the world. Lord, but I loved to watch that man brawl. He was the wrong body type to fight as a true heavyweight, had the frame of a one-hundred-seventy-five pounder, in fact, but he was a fearless warrior.

The sports press called him Bump because he was always bumping into his opponents, usually with his head or a well-placed elbow that flashed from nowhere and never failed to land on an exposed chin or cheekbone. Some boxing observers contended he fought dirty, but I disagreed. In the fight game, rules are pretty much for athletic commissions and amateurs. Bump Boyer was a helluva brawler, and I made plenty of money off him in several fights for the very reason that, in the late rounds with everything on the line, he could be counted on to give his all.

"You're Bump Boyer," I said simply.

"Yeah, could you believe it? I'm trying to sell some gold but the cheap sonofabitch don't want my stuff."

He held a small baggy in his big mitt. I could not tell what it contained.

"Pawnbrokers can be fickle."

"You're telling me. I've been coming to this place and the Super Ace for years to sell a few things that have come my way, and never had no problems. But this Jew guy, lately he's got problems with every move I make. Talks about the price of gold not being what it used to be. And now he's threatened to call the cops if I don't go and never come back."

"Fortunately, there are plenty of other shops in Las Vegas."

An aching feeling began to fill the pit of my stomach. It's the feeling I sometimes get when I'm being played.

"Yeah, but I was looking for some fast cash. I've got a few things working that need immediate attention, and I don't have time to travel around shopping for a decent deal. I just need a couple hundred and I'm set. Besides, the material is top-quality gold. Trouble is, the Jew won't deal. I know he buys scrap and has it melted down. But he don't want my stuff."

"I wish I could help you, Bump, but"

"Maybe you can," he said, suddenly smiling. "I just need a couple hundred and the material is good. I know it is, because I know where it come from."

"Well, unfortunately, I really don't have the means to help you, Bump, although I would if I could," I said, watching his face go from sunny to partly cloudy. "I sure enjoyed watching you in the ring. You were a helluva fighter with the biggest heart I ever saw, and I've seen the greatest of the last fifty years."

He just nodded.

"Can't eat appreciation," he said. "Know what I'm saying? I've got a family to support, mouths to feed, rent to pay. I've got obligations just like everybody else. Appreciation don't pay my bills."

I shrugged, feeling the heat of whatever mania was stalking his battered brain. Before I could leave he asked, "At least take a look at my goods? You haven't even looked at my stuff."

He opened the baggy and said, "Hold out your hand." He emptied the contents of the bag and I watched as sixteen gold teeth filled my palm. Dried blood still stained them.

"Picked them up from a guy cheap," Bump Boyer said, flashing his very white teeth. "Several guys, actually. They all said they wasn't using them, so I could have them."

"That's quite a coincidence," I said, thanking my good fortune as I ran my tongue over my own silver fillings. I tried my best to keep my hand from quivering.

"Ain't it the truth? Anyway, you sure you can't make use of them? I'll sell them for ten cents on the dollar."

"I'm positive," I said, making certain every tooth wound up back in the baggy. "I wear dentures, myself."

Bump Boyer laughed loud at that one.

"Turns out, so do the guys who used to own these," he said, flashing a smile that haunted my thoughts the rest of the day.

Money Ahead

Those who had the misfortune of knowing him called him Tommy Mooch. His real name is Mucelli, but with Tommy no one bothered with the proper pronunciation.

Tommy was so used to the name that he didn't correct people. The truth was, Mooch fit Tommy like a tailored shirt.

When I first met him at Del Mar many years ago, I called him Two-Dollar Tommy because he was always hitting me up for two bucks to play a horse.

"Got a hunch, don't need a bunch," he'd say.

In those days I was pretty flush, so a couple of bucks meant nothing to me. Tommy was a war veteran who wore a prosthesis up to his knee. As I'm a sucker for a peg leg, I gave the guy a break.

Little did I know that Tommy had a regular route he worked like a mailman. He put 50 miles on that bum leg every race day. For all I know he had a hundred guys at the track he nicked for two bucks. I heard he paid a guy back once, but it turned out to be a vicious rumor.

Years passed, I fell on harder times and ended up coming home to Las Vegas, where I took an apartment downtown and managed my bankroll by betting at Leroy's and Mel Exber's place. I was happy to live out the remainder of my years as a small-timer.

Out of the blue who should show up downtown but Tommy Mooch. I can't say I was happy to see him standing between me and the door of Leroy's Horse and Sports Place. Tommy, of course, knew that the first race of the day started in less than ten minutes and I'd want to keep our conversation brief in order to place my ten-dollar exacta. Hearing that cloying greeting and that simpering set-up line after a few years was nauseating.

"Jasper, old man, you're looking good," Tommy said, proceeding to tell me of his exploits in California, where he claimed he'd run a game at one of the big poker clubs and had been in fat city for two years before experiencing a minor tax beef.

For Tommy, it was a genuinely creative yarn, downright dramatic compared with his usual hang-dog shoulder shrug and eyes focused on his shoes.

"But I'm coming back strong," Tommy said. "Got a good line on some inside dope at Hollywood Park, a guy whose brother is a top assistant behind the scenes."

"You mean a stable boy, Tommy?" I asked, feeling him inch closer. A con always likes to violate your personal space. "Some kid who, like yourself, has mastered the art of shoveling horse manure. Am I right?"

"Same old Jasper, always making with the wisecracks," Tommy whined. "I'm on the square, I swear. He's got good information, but"

"But you don't have a nickel to test that information," I said.

Tommy was in check. I could hear the wheel in his hamster cage of a brain squeaking.

"Hey, I know it's good stuff. The kid's legit. He loves me like a brother. And he hears things. I talked to him yesterday. He told me they was holding back a certain two-year-old favorite, and the owners of said favorite were placing a large sum on an eighteen-to-one shot, which means I've got the best of it. It's the closest thing to steam going."

"All you need is something to put down."

He shrugged his narrow shoulders, studied the cigarette butts at his feet.

Then I had a sidewalk epiphany. I pulled out my wallet and picked a twenty-dollar bill from my slender bankroll and held it in front of his face. Tommy appeared on the verge of drooling.

"See Mr. Jackson, Tommy?"

He nodded.

"Mr. Jackson is important to me. He's a big man on my small campus, as it were. He's yours on one condition."

"What's that?"

"That you return him in one piece. Not a buck at a time, not five today and catch you later. In one bill. Agreed?"

"But I only wanted two bucks, a fin tops."

"I don't want to give you two bucks, or five. I want to give you twenty. As long as we're in agreement on the conditions of the loan."

He hesitated, thinking of the ramifications.

Using the sixth sense that all degenerate horse players have, he felt that the first race of the day was only moments away. Something had to give.

At last Tommy Mooch relented. He took my twenty in his left hand, moved it directly into his pants pocket. Checkmate.

"My old pal, Jasper," he said, his eyes not making contact with mine. "I'll get this back to you today."

"Of course you will."

With that, he turned and slipped inside Leroy's. Knowing I was money ahead, I decided to stroll over to the Las Vegas Club to celebrate.

I never saw him again.

WESTSIDE LUCK

His name was William George Washington, but everyone in the department called him Willie Bear. He was a cop on the old City P.D. before it consolidated with the Sheriff's Office to make the Metropolitan Police Department. He was the biggest, blackest human being I had ever seen. And he was my friend.

Willie Bear went nearly four-hundred pounds and was no less than six foot six. His uniforms had to be specially made, and he had difficulty wedging himself behind the wheel of the police cruiser. For many years he was a kickass cop with a Westside chip on his shoulder. He had something to prove to his people, and maybe to a department that was almost exclusively white.

Willie was a fearless stomper of street hoodlums, gang-bangers, and gold-toothed pimps. Drug bars cleared out when Willie walked in. The corner of H and Jackson was as quiet as a church on the nights he worked.

Working undercover was out of the question for Willie, but for many years he was a good cop who wanted nothing more than to clean up the streets near where his wife and nine children lived. This was back in the day when we believed such things were possible. We didn't know any better.

Back then, Willie's only vice was eating. I was a rookie when I met him and was his partner four years. In that time I saw him consume such copious amounts of food that I can scarcely relate it. He was the original buffet buster, who could swallow five pounds of ham in a sitting and then stare lovingly at the dessert display.

We worked swings on the Westside and had a nightly ritual. Unless we were on a felony call, no matter what we were doing we dropped it a few minutes before eleven and sped to the Kentucky Fried Chicken on Rancho Drive. The chicken shop's high school employees were just closing up for the night.

I can't imagine what they do with their leftovers now, but in those years the manager didn't keep the cooked chicken overnight. They got rid of it, sometimes heaping trays of the stuff. If the workers haven't grown sick of smelling chicken with seven herbs and spices and plenty of oil all day, they could take home a bag. Ideally, of course, they are supposed to cook just enough chicken to complete the night's orders, but frying chicken isn't an exact science.

Willie ate the leftovers. Not all of them, just a dozen or so pieces to get him through the night. He took the rest in a bag, maybe thirty pieces in all, home to his wife and kids.

Almost every night for four years, like clockwork, come five minutes to eleven Willie would be at the back of the KFC pounding on the door. The school kids who answered the door never questioned him. He was bigger than the giant bucket that spun atop a pole in the parking lot. It was a form of graft, I guess, but I never looked at it that way. A lot of guys were taking a lot more than chicken in those days.

"They just gonna throw it out," he would say, offering me a piece as we drove away. I was only good for a leg.

"You're doing them a favor," I'd reply. "And the way you eat, without that chicken your kids would starve."

I'm not the best judge of ethics, having run into my own income tax troubles after I retired from the department. Ray Chester never was good with numbers, as my divorce settlements illustrate. But I can vouch for Willie in those days. He was one of the straightest beat cops in the department. Working in his own neighborhood, he had temptations that were lost on others. He knew every heroin dealer and pimp daddy on the alphabet streets. Even as a rookie I could see he wasn't in anyone's pocket. He took chicken from the Colonel, but he wouldn't accept a nickel from one of the smacked-up streetwalkers. Pimps didn't pay him, unless they liked paying for an ass whipping.

• • •

It's easy for a man to say he'd never go on someone's pad. Chances are good they've never been two months behind on their mortgage, had a sick kid and crappy insurance, or ever got an offer of a month's pay for simply looking the other way in a town that thrives on looking the other way. For a long while, Willie was a mountain of strength.

Then came the call on the police cruiser radio that one of his kids was at the county hospital. We'd only dropped off the chicken at his house a couple hours earlier. Kid got up in the middle of the night for a snack and choked on one of the bones. By the time we got to the hospital, she was gone.

We stood in the lobby of the emergency room, which was littered with the usual poor faces, overdose cases, and drunks looking for three hots and a cot. The gun-and-knife club victims took up most of the doctors' attention. The rest had to wait their turn.

"I couldn't get that old car started," his wife Sherlyn said through her tears. "I called for the ambulance, but it didn't come for almost an hour."

Willie was staggered by her words.

"But you're a cop's wife. Did you tell them that?"

"They didn't believe me," she said. "They only believed the address."

• • •

After the funeral, Willie returned to work. He was quiet as you might expect, and he was still a professional on the beat. But where we'd once been able to fill the cruiser with laughter or family stories, the swing shift passed in silence broken only by the dispatcher's voice on the radio.

Within a year I transferred to the detective division. We said our goodbyes with a handshake, and I left him working the neighborhoods he'd known his whole life. I said I'd keep in touch, but we didn't see much of each other after that. I drank with the detectives when my shift ended, let the job wreck the first of my three marriages, and felt my feet get flatter by the day.

Don't get me wrong. I liked police work. It was in my blood. But it grinds your soul to cigarette ash. It reminds you every day what a cesspool the world can be. Some guys cling to religion, others grip the bottle for strength, a few end up eating their gun.

A surprising number of pretty good cops take solace in the shadow between light and dark. They take comps and tips from pimps and drug dealers. They start living at topless bars and dating the dancers, or hanging in wiseguy restaurants and wearing pinkie rings. They find real estate deals and side jobs working security. They moonlight as private detectives or sell case information out the back door. They build houses with heavily discounted materials and flip them for profit. Or they develop enough dirt on rich country clubbers and squeeze them for a little spending money. Some even become politicians.

By the time Willie got fired for taking protection money from a drug dealer who ran a cocktail lounge on Jackson, I wasn't a bit surprised. I felt a little sorry for him. Privately, I even suspected I knew the turning point in his life that changed him. But what are you going to do?

Just a few years back Willie did a short hitch in the state penitentiary for drugs, and the last time I saw him he was acting as a lookout and bodyguard for a crack dealer. He'd lost so much weight I didn't recognize him. He weighed maybe 170 pounds. He recognized me and said hello with the rotten teeth of a crack pipe junkie.

I was back in uniform, getting ready to retire, and frankly didn't have the heart to hassle him. I knew it wasn't drugs that had ruined his appetite.

Good News

They say newspapers never print enough good news, but just the other day Crazy Charlie showed up at the door of my apartment, my copy of the local rag in his filthy hands, to explain that he knew all about one of the stories found on the front page of the local section.

Crazy Charlie's not as crazy as he seems. He uses the talking-to-Jesus patter to augment his career as a downtown window washer. Charlie doesn't do the high-rises. He approaches your car when it's trapped at the light and starts spraying until you're paying him a buck to go away.

It hasn't done a thing for his personal hygiene, which I've taken issue with over the years. (At one point as a joke I gave him a bar of soap for Christmas and told him that despite what he'd heard, it wouldn't bite.) But Charlie does all right, collecting enough to augment his Social Security to keep himself in a studio apartment with enough leftover to pay for the vodka he drinks.

He is not, however, flush enough to afford his own subscription to the local rag, which arrives on my doorstep each morning about five. As we are both old men, we are awake at five. Me with my second cup of coffee, and Charlie with his second blast of potato drippings. I sometimes catch him reading the sections before me, his greasy hands smudging the pages as he thumbs through the sparse international news to the local stories and sports. He gets sheepish and quickly reassembles the paper, saying he'll come back later when I'm finished.

But on this morning he was standing straight, holding up the local section after banging on my door like a SWAT sergeant.

"Get a look at this, Crabbe," he said. "I made the news."

"Obituaries?"

"Very funny. I'll outlive you and give you odds."

"You'll be well preserved from the formaldehyde you drink."

"Handsome, too. But look at this story."

He pointed to a headline that read, "Accused Coach Dies in Jail."

•••

The story was about a local Little League baseball coach who'd been accused of molesting his players. It was a scandal here not too long ago, in part because the coach was one of those phony religious types who wore his hair short, kept his Bible quotes handy, served as a lieutenant in his church and coerced children into performing sex acts in his spare time. In short, the kind of guy who deserved to have his worthless predator's life snuffed like a roach, but probably would get plenty of therapy and a segregated cell at the state penitentiary. Only the finest accommodations for our snitches and baby rapers.

But the Clark County Detention Center is overcrowded, and its segregated cellblock is stuffed beyond capacity. So those waiting for trial are sometimes mixed with the general population.

Which is how the coach met one of his former players, Crazy Charlie told me.

"I was in on a disorderly sitting on a bench right next to this bull-necked, tattooed guy, one of those kids who looks like he ate a bowl of steroids for breakfast, when I see the coach sit down. He's recognizable from your morning paper, and the bull does a double take, then does something that makes me cringe. He smiles.

"Well, the two start making small talk, and I figure the big muscle-bound guy is really one of those Gentle Ben types. Because you never know who's who inside.

"Over the weekend, I see them talking close, like they were conspiring a breakout or planning their wedding. Then last night, about twenty minutes before I'm scheduled to leave, it happened.

"The bull suddenly raises his voice and picks the coach up by the neck.

"'Now do you remember me?' he shouts. "'I'm Eddie Rowe. I played right field and couldn't catch a ball.'

"It got uglier from there. The bull slammed the coach's head into the wall again and again. We all moved to the far end of the cell. I mean everybody. Muslims, Mexicans, piss bums and lifers. This kid was certifiable. In a few minutes it was over. There was blood all over the wall and the coach's head turned to mush. He was dead as disco.

"It took time for the guards to arrive. I hadn't noticed at first, but one of the bull's friends had put a wad of gum over the lens of the cell's surveillance camera.

"I spent an extra couple of hours in lockdown, but it was worth it. Turned out nobody saw a thing.

"When it was my turn to give a statement I told them to leave it up to Jesus. Surely he'd know a man's heart and judge him accordingly."

With that, Crazy Charlie grinned and we old men with our own scars clanked our cups in celebration.

TANYA AND GACY

Tanya believed that anyone who was serious about dancing had to have a gimmick. Not an act, exactly, for there weren't many real fan-dancing strippers left working the topless clubs in Las Vegas or Hollywood, but something more than just a surgically enhanced set of breasts and a willingness to show them off.

Although plastic surgeons were probably more responsible for the increased popularity of topless cabarets than the mob or the dot-com boomers, Tanya told herself the trade was about more than boobs and booze.

Tanya's thing was the baby-doll look. She wore a cute little diaper, carried a big lollipop and a pacifier. The whole bit.

At twenty-two, she was petite and pretty close to flat-chested with a face that looked ready for the first day of junior high school. She had little education and no family, but a desire to care for her three-year-old son, Sundance Cassidy. And so she skipped the G.E.D. and beautician school route, passed up the Burger King apprenticeship and the telemarketing tryout, and proceeded right to Mr. Rick's Cabaret, where the day manager took one look at her and shook his head. He double- and triple-checked her driver's license and work card setup to make sure she was street legal, then put her to work during the heart of the construction worker lunch hour. If that didn't scare her away, nothing would.

She was a tough kid, all eighty pounds of her. She was quick with a smile and quicker with a slap at a roaming hand. Even with the club's draconian kickback system, where everyone in the house from the doorman to the bossman gets zooked before a dancer clears her first dollar, Tanya started making what for her seemed like big money.

Within a few weeks she moved with Sundance into a two-bedroom apartment and hired a nanny.

The baby-doll thing was pretty popular. Of course she had to put up with the endlessly suggestive talk from the customers, but she'd expected that. If they were talking, chances were good they were tipping.

John Wayne Gacy made her change her mind.

Not the actual Gacy, mind you, for he'd finally been put to sleep by the state for the killing of thirty-three young boys, but a pudgy shoe salesman named Earl who could have passed for Gacy's twin.

He started coming in every day just to see Tanya, have her give him a twenty-dollar table dance, when he invariably started breathing too hard and moaning like a bitch in heat. It was pretty freaky stuff, but by then Tanya had convinced herself she had a kid at home to think about. The money, even Gacy's money, was too good to pass up.

And he only stayed an hour or so. Then he waddled back into the late-afternoon light, and Tanya shuddered and wanted a shower. She talked to Tommy, the day bouncer, about him and asked him to keep an eye out, but it didn't change the fact he was a good customer who hadn't really done anything wrong.

Then came the day Gacy stayed all day and asked for Tanya exclusively. His pockets bulged with bills and he ordered dance after dance. Always moaning. Always breathing hard. Never quite touching her, but managing to give her the shivering creeps.

At one point he opened his eyes and noticed the goose bumps on her arms. He smiled lasciviously, breathed in deep through his nostrils.

It was then Tanya realized what Gacy was up to. He wasn't the usual horny cement finisher on his lunch hour who wanted to drink a few beers, talk dirty and maybe cop a feel.

It was her fear of him and maybe the scent of her son that turned him on. He'd managed to slip beneath the veneer of cold professionalism all dancers wear like makeup. He'd scared her, chilled her to the bone, and he could barely contain himself.

On the other hand, it was nearly three p.m. and Tanya checked her kitty. Gacy had slipped her more than a thousand dollars in twenties in under four hours.

She smiled down at the fat, quivering freak and excused herself. He stayed slouched in his chair, awaiting her return and waving away cocktail waitresses.

It was ten after two. Tanya grabbed an early out, leaving through the side exit. In thirty minutes, she was showered and home with her Sundance.

Back at Rick's Cabaret, by three p.m. Gacy had suffi-
ciently gathered his wits to ask Tommy the day bouncer
where his favorite baby doll had gone.

"She left an hour ago," Tommy said, scowling. "Maybe
you should come back tomorrow and try again."

At home, innocent son in her arms, Tanya thought
seriously about getting another gimmick.

Thinking Nickels

I suspect Bev and Marty are newcomers to Las Vegas. Not tourists, mind you, but retirement-age locals of limited residential experience.

How do I know their names?

That's easy. They are embroidered on their matching red silk poker jackets, the backs of which advertise a local's casino known for its large video poker payouts. Although their green caps are not embroidered, they advertise a different locals casino, which also is proud of its liberal video poker jackpots. It's a wonder some casino marketing genius doesn't question their loyalties.

Turns out the machines at these competing casinos pay out up to an amazing one-hundred-ten percent. Not to mention all the generous clothing and buffet comps for players. It's a wonder these casino people stay in business. Yeah, you bet it is.

I'm standing in line behind Bev and Marty at the Fiesta buffet and watching them attempt to balance enough fried chicken, lasagna, egg rolls, ham, trout almandine, roast beef and potatoes and gravy to feed Yugoslavia. Is it lunch for two, or an Osmond family picnic?

They are so overloaded their plate-side thumbs are completely obscured. Although they risk leaving a trail of gravy from the carving station to the dice pit, it leaves them free hands to palm slices of pie and brownies on their way back to home base.

Most Las Vegas veterans know it's smarter to go back for seconds than it is to risk a hernia and public mortification lifting a plated loaded down with enough artery-clogging chuck to dam the mighty Mississippi.

I make a nice salad with diet Italian dressing, add a couple of artichoke hearts, and return to my seat, which, as chance would have it, is next to the table for four occupied by Bev and Marty. Between bites and deep guttural whispers and groans of digestive delight, they discuss the day's agenda.

"I'm feeling quarters, Bev," Marty says.

"Quarters?" asks Bev. "Are you sure? Quarters?"

"Quarters, Bev."

"I don't know, Marty. You said quarters last time."

"Last time was nickels and one roll of quarters."

"No, I distinctly remember you saying quarters. I think I might have talked you out of quarters, except for the one roll, but I know you felt quarters."

"Well, I've feeling quarters today, Bev. Really, I am. A gut feeling."

"I don't know, Marty. I'm thinking nickels. Nickels are where we need to be today. Our money management has been pretty lackluster since the big one in January."

"The big one was sweet, wasn't it?"

"Extremely sweet. Drawing the ace of hearts to complete the royal was one to write home about, but that was in

January, Martin, and it's been busted flushes since then. You know what I mean."

"You don't have to tell me."

"You promised, no more credit cards, no more dipping into our principal. No more double-up to catch up."

"I know, honey. I know. But I have to tell you. I'm really feeling quarters today. I've never had this kind of feeling. Not even in January when I hit the royal. Then I was feeling good about it, but not like this. I know our luck is turning, honey. I swear to God I know it. We'll be right back where we were, and I promise I'll make the principal right again."

"Because you know we're not exactly ready for the graveyard, Marty. We have to manage our money, just like in the book. 'Manage your money, and have fun,' that's what the book said. 'Don't forget the risk-reward ratio, and have fun.' Remember?"

"Of course I remember. I read the book first. It was me who gave you the book for Christmas. You don't have to tell me about the book. I know what the book says."

"Well, then let's go by the book."

"But the book say to have fun, and I know we'll have fun if we play quarters today. I'm telling you, Bev honey, I'm feeling quarters."

"But I'm thinking nickels, sweetie. At least until we level off a bit."

They returned to their plates, and for a while all that could be heard was the distant jingling of jackpots. I was nearly finished with my salad.

Then Marty said, "How about a compromise, honey? We'll play quarters for one hour, then we'll switch to nickels no matter where we're at. We'll cash out and spend the rest of the day with the nickels. No matter what. I promise."

"Are you sure you really feel it this time?"

"I swear, honey. I swear I feel it."

"Well, all right. But I'm still thinking nickels."

Produce

He was old. Not merely graying at the temples or a certified senior citizen, but almost as old as the dust that clotted on the window sills of his studio apartment downtown. He had liked to tell his neighbors, back when his neighbors spoke English, that he was as old as the state of Arizona and twice as prickly. But he wasn't so prickly, of course. Those neighbors knew he was just a lonely old man who drank too much jug wine and never stopped talking about the old Las Vegas and his glory years with his wife, Ruthie, and the old Desert Inn.

"'Wilbur Clark's Desert Inn,' in those days," he would say. "I was a trusted floorman, and Ruthie ran cocktails. Oh, she had the legs of a chorus girl, but she was smart enough not to fall in with the show crowd. We made a good living between us and witnessed Las Vegas history as it was made. Not by Wilbur Clark, of course, but by Mr. Moe Dalitz and his pals from Cleveland and Chicago. They took a liking to me because I was from Cleveland, the outskirts of Shaker Heights, actually, but close enough for these guys. Moe was something else. If you didn't know better, you'd think he was just another little Jewish guy with two bucks in his pocket. Absolutely unpretentious. Never put no heat on anybody, never threw his weight around. He was all class in my book."

Over time the old man retired, then lost his Ruthie to lung cancer, then moved out of the family home off Paradise Road to a more practical apartment, then eventually to the studio in the heart of downtown's immigrant district. He didn't mind the changing faces so much as the fact that there was no one to talk to, no one to share his theory of life with.

As time passed, he'd little by little lost the things that had been dear to him. Then those physical abilities faded that had seemed so important at one time. His sight, hearing, the spring in his step, and his sex drive. He and Ruthie had had a pretty good sex life. He'd been loyal to her over fifty-two years, cheating on her once in a fit of frustration but regretting it. He'd managed to retain his sense of smell, but little more. He was, after all, eighty-eight years old.

"As many years as keys on a piano," he told a waitress at the cafe he frequented for poached eggs on toast.

The old man spent more time reliving his life in the casino business, but when he got out he took the CAT bus to the Smith's supermarket. He would spend the next three hours slowly pushing his cart up and down the aisles. He was still too proud to use a walker, and this enabled him to get out without the risk of falling and breaking anything important.

He'd start at one end of the store, deli, meats and seafood, and work his way through the bread aisle, past the pasta and canned goods, pet products, pop, dairy, frozen foods and all the way to the produce department. The Promised Land. The selection of fruits and vegetables was not expansive at the store, but quite adequate, and the old man savored every stop along the way. He held a sample of each piece of fruit up to his nose and inhaled fresh scents and memories.

The apples, especially the galas, reminded him of fall afternoons in childhood. The oranges, of mornings at the beach in Florida with Ruthie, ordering from room service after sleeping in late.

Then the memories were mixed with more primal feelings. The skin of the nectarines and peaches was fresh and supple, like that of a young woman. He always bought one of each to take home and smell that sweet youth in privacy.

The grapefruit filled his hand like a firm breast, and he blushed at his daydream. There were the firm cucumbers and the pungent onions and the intoxicating flush that overwhelmed his sense of smell with fresh rosemary and basil.

He saved his favorite, the California avocados, for last. How he reveled in discovering a ripe one. The skins of the avocados went through such a dramatic metamorphosis in such a short time, from smooth and supple to deep-lined and rugged, that he found himself admiring them. He knew he would eat a ripe one for dinner when he returned home.

His routine rarely varied. He was playing out the string of his days alone. But on shopping days he would hesitate to consider himself a lonely old man. Not with so many fresh scents filling his small apartment. Not with the touch and taste of life and love so close at hand.

AFTERGLOW

t was after. I was still trying to get my bearings, as this sort of thing takes more out of me than it used to.

As is my habit, a playfully perverse one to be sure, I clicked on the tape recorder I kept secured behind the headboard and waited for the inevitable small talk that followed the business at hand.

She finished washing up in the hotel bathroom and returned to sit on the edge of the bed while she dressed. The financial transaction, as ever, had been taken care of ahead of time, and in a few minutes she would return back into the night. I never felt melancholy or even put off by the businesslike manner of prostitutes. Frankly, I liked watching them dress almost as much as seeing them disrobe.

We had entered the netherworld between the sex and the sayonara. Strange as it may seem, it was the time I looked forward to most. It was the awkward moment when the truth of the transaction would become a lie we both could live with, me knowing that she was an emotional cripple, and her knowing that I was a lonely old man.

It went this way:

"Feeling refreshed?" I started.

"Absolutely, honey," she said. "I'm practically knocked out. You're something else. When I first saw you, I have to be honest, my hopes weren't high, but you surprised me. You're like, seventy, right? I know guys half your age who don't have your stamina. Believe me. And you're a gentleman, which I appreciate.

"There's no such thing as a gentleman under fifty. Men are pigs until they're fifty. Some are pigs forever, of course, but it takes until they're fifty before they learn how to treat a girl. You're special in that way, I mean it. You can call me as often as you want, love.

"That's really what I want, a few generous friends like you and to quit the service, which believe me has really gotten old. I don't work that much, just a day a week and on weekends. I can't give up weekends, the money's fantastic and it gives me plenty of time to be with my kid. I really don't do this all that much anymore. I have a couple girls I work with, and we do parties for conventions and high-rollers, that sort of thing.

"It's very good money. And it's enabled me to invest well. If everything works out, I'll be able to get out of the business in a year. Then I'll be able to afford to go back to school, complete my business degree, and move into something new. I've been dancing and entertaining for almost ten years."

"It doesn't show," I said.

"Aren't you sweet? Well, I can tell, and I'm getting to the age when I need to think about doing something else. It's not easy to walk away from the money, but I'm working on paying off a few debts and moving to the next level, you know what I mean?"

"Exactly."

"That's the thing about Las Vegas. People don't realize how big the business is here. They look in the phone book and see the escort ads, but that's just a fraction of the real business. I mean, I know girls who dance at the clubs and they make 200, 300 thousand a year. And it's not like they're declaring every nickel to Uncle Sam. So they're doing really well, but they're like twentysomething and it's all going to their boyfriends or up their noses or for clothes and a Porsche, or something really intelligent like that. They don't realize that nothing lasts forever. Not the big money, and not their looks.

"Well, it took a few hard lessons, but I've learned mine. I've set the clock and I'm keeping to my schedule and my business plan. I'm doing my parties and investing the money. One of the advantages of this business is that some gentlemen want to help you with finances. I get more stock tips than a Wall Street broker. And they're not all puffed-up pillow talk. I've done well with them. I have a financial planner working with me, investing in a diversified portfolio that combines a little risk with enough stability to ride out this bear market. Bear market, nothing. This is a recession we're in."

"But you seem to be doing all right."

Having finished dressing, she stood on long legs and adjusted her short skirt.

She smiled at me and said, "Sweetheart, some professions are recession-proof."

The Hat

What was it Solly was saying?

"There's worse deaths than fifty a shift and the occasional tip on a horse. You'll live."

Yeah, but when you're used to earning and playing and sleeping late, it's almost like being dead standing behind the counter taking suckers' money and watching them bet the wrong way—upside down and backwards—every single time. It's safe, sure, but where's the angle? That's the trouble with the straight game, playing it square. No pulse. Safe as Sunday school, but it's got no heartbeat.

Guy a minute ago wanted to play two-hundred on Notre Dame and give up five touchdowns against Army. Maybe he knows Notre Dame's quarterback won't start, ankle sprain, maybe he don't. Don't matter. Guy's a fan, a diehard alumni with a Fighting Irish jacket to prove it and a class ring on his right hand. We could have set the number at fifty and he still would have taken the Irish. Wouldn't dream of betting against his team. Bets with his heart, not his head. Guy's a sucker.

Deal is, the way the Irish have the luck this season, he could end up cashing that ticket. But that don't make him wise.

Six months of watching other people make idiot bets has got me itchy. Six months and nothing, no calls, no

messages, nothing. It's like the lights went out in Chicago.
I started thinking they got no phones in Chicago, or maybe
somebody forgot about me. Solly don't like to use phones,
it's understandable. But a post card or a letter with a hang
in there, kid or something would be nice. Something. Just
to tell me he remembers I'm sitting here quietly rotting
away in the Desert Palm Casino sports book, not making any trips to Rudy's, not knocking around with any of
the guys. I'm as stiff as a wooden Indian. Straight game
is like having a bad cold.

Not that I'm some kind of operator, mind you. That
would be the wrong impression to get. I like the life, that's
all. Never wanted to be the mayor or the governor or the
king of France. I just like to watch ballgames and bet
horses and drink whiskey and chase women and sleep
late. There's no harm in that, is there? Except, you won't
be surprised to learn, not too many people will pay you
to bet ballgames and horses. So you've got to earn if you
want to play. It's like Solly says, "It's a jungle out there.
You got to decide whether you're going to eat or be eaten."

I guess I like to eat as well as the next guy, but, you
know, I don't like my steaks blood rare. Maybe that's why
some of the fellas don't take me too serious. And maybe
that's why my name don't show up in the papers or on
anybody's list of unsavories. Maybe that's why Solly gave
me the nod and not some other guy. I like to have my
fun, and I know when to shut up and listen, but I don't
like to attract attention to myself. That's why this goes
no further than us, all right?

Besides, I ain't said nothing serious. And, anyway, I'm playing the straight game right now, so there's nothing to it.

It's a little like being invited to a big meal, say a huge spread, and being forced to sit with your hands folded, holding your breath until the damn dinner prayer is finished or you get whacked by your old man with a backhand across the face. Nothing stings quite like it. Man, I tell you I can almost feel the fist of hunger clench in my gut and make my stomach moan like a cat in an alley.

This is a cash town. Old guys with three days' growth o beard carry more in a clip in their front pockets than some straight guys can earn in a year. Hell, it's nothing to see someonepull out three inches of folded cash, most of it C notes. A guy wants to flash ten or fifteen grand in a Las Vegas sports book, there ain't nothing to it. That ain't deep pockets in a cash town like this one.

So there's always guys getting in too deep, riding that fourth-place finish all the way to the shark tank. That's where I come in, but that's nothing but a sideline. It's an investment, is all it is, something that needs ground work and maintenance. Simple, really, as long as you don't get sloppy. The state's got no shylock statute, so you can charge the going rate to anyone who will take it. You can't say no threats, but you can make sure a guy gets the message.

My game has been mostly outside. Booking is a job. Betting's a drug. I like to bring in food from Los Angeles, steaks and chops and booze and lobsters when I can get them. I had a dozen bars and restaurants by myself who would take all I could deliver, but that was before Solly told us to knock off the mischief until the summer cooled down. Now it's the fall, and I'm into a loanshark myself. Nothing heavy, nothing I can't handle, a few hundred a week juice, and I can produce that from air. Don't ask why I don't earn right from behind the sports book window. That would be a stupid question.

Had a pro boxer once for about a year and a half. Dreamed of becoming a ringside big shot. Worst move I ever made in my life. Kid was a white kid, Irish kid named Maloney. You never heard of him. Here I am figuring a good white kid who can punch a little and keep his chin down can go far in this town. Fight fans want whites to win no matter who's the champ. What I didn't know is my middleweight dreamed of being a heavyweight. Ate like two pregnant women. Got one fight in six months and went three rounds before some Mexican kid opens him up like a cantaloupe on the forehead and then buries him with shots to the gut. I put easy five grand into him and I might as well of flushed it, the good it did me. He was the best fed middleweight in the history of the division, but back then the five large didn't dent my bankroll. It was mostly embarrassing, me buying two dozen tickets and standing around like a proud father with all the guys sitting there and then listening to them laugh their asses off when the punk collapses. I coulda killed him myself. Now I'm just a spectator as far as boxing goes. It's cheaper.

Lately, of course, that five grand would be a welcomed sight. Sometimes I can't believe I fiddled it away on the Maloney kid. Fat bunch of nothing lower is what he was.

I never should have stole him out from under Johnny Tocco. At a grand, I figured he was a bargain. The old man isn't as old as I thought he was.

Now five grand would be a sizable bankroll for me. That's the way it is. I never been good at saving. Money talks to me when it's in my pocket, and it don't shut up until it's in someone else's. Don't get me wrong. I'm no sucker. I'm wise enough. But if you play, sooner or later you're going to pay. That's just the way the game is. And I love to watch the horses run.

There's something about them that's beautiful. That they can earn for you is part of it, but there's something about the track and the parade of ponies that I really like. When they lose, of course, I like it a lot less.

So, anyway, I'm standing behind the counter Tuesday afternoon trying not to snicker at the sucker a hundred on the Lakers minus seven against the Spurs when the hat catches my eye. Bobbing through the players in the back of the book, it's blue and gray and cut at a wicked tilt. Solly D.

I hand the player his ticket, wished him all the best, and caught a glimpse of the hat through two tourists squinting at the big board. When they parted, he was standing in the back with his arms crossed, staring right at me like he'd been waiting for me to notice him. He smiled. Me, too. He raised two fingers, then covers his right eye with one hand. I nod: Rudy's, two hours. For those of you who don't know, Rudy wears an eye patch ever since a coke freak carved on it with a knife. But you wouldn't know this unless you been there.

Imagine that, Solly D. right there in the back of the book. I could hardly believe my eyes. Suddenly, I could feel my heart beating again. I could hardly wait two hours for the shift change. It was like the fog was lifting or something. Solly did good work. When he came up with a caper, it paid a big return. That's why he was still out there when the Little Guy and Lefty were long gone. There was a reason why he had me standing behind the counter for six months. It was bound to be something good with Solly back in town. With him back, I know the straight game is about to end.

LOSING EDDIE

A guy's got maybe no friends in this world, and when he's low and walking all night that's as sure a bet as any. But I always had Eddie, and a truer friend I never had, and I'm sure things would be looking better if only I could find him.

He vanished only a couple days ago, but Eddie and me go way back before that. We started as friends a few days after I got here. He was a pup laying low alongside his brothers and sisters under this dumpster downtown. They was dead, and there ain't many things sadder than dead puppies, but Eddie was still sitting there moving his brown head forth and back and trying to stay comfortable near his family. I don't know where his mama run off to, but she was long gone down some alley maybe looking for food or maybe picked up by the pound or hit by a car or something. Gone, anyway. That's sure enough.

It's hot even in the early morning when I like to get up and check out around the back of the little Italian place downtown for leftovers and bread. It's not a bad way to start the day. I never liked the mess hall on Bonanza: Some good guys to play cards with, but too many bums and too much preaching about finding and saving your soul. Hell, I know where my soul is. I just don't know where my next meal is and my next job is. It ain't all that difficult to figure out even in hot weather.

I'm almost to the Italian back door when I see him under the dumpster sticking his little head out. And, ah man, I couldn't say no to them eyes. He was about gone when I picked him up and the smell of his brothers and sisters was about all anybody could stand, but I scooped him up and washing him in the spigot off to the side of the building. They take the little twister off the spigot, but I carry a pair of pliers in my pocket just for that reason. They also come in handy when one of the loonies comes around asking for donations to put Jesus through college.

Well, this pup perks right up and drinks so much of the water he about bloats. He's making wee all over the alley and in a few minutes his curly tail is wagging. Then he starts yapping like I'm stepping on him, and Jesus I know what that means cause I'd yapped enough in the last few weeks myself. The little fella's hungry.

Hey, me too, so I get my footing and hoist myself into the dumpster and as always there's the good morning greeting from a gang of roaches and Jap beetles the size of Snickers bars. They tickle your legs and that just about scares the water out of you and makes you want to scream like a schoolgirl the first time it happens. It happens almost every time down there, but I still can't get used to it.

After a fair amount of fishing I come up with about four clean fistfuls of cold spaghetti and enough half-eaten meatballs to make a good-sized meatloaf. That's good enough. And the garlic bread, more than half a loaf in all, is even better. I could go and get a forty-nine-cent breakfast at the Nevada and sip coffee until they throw me out, but I've got about five bucks to my name before I start cruising grocery stores, and I've never been too good at stealing, so I decide to stick to the alleys and a few friendly misplaced link sausages on toast one of the fry cooks at the Fremont hands me outside the kitchen doors.

What does the pup think of all this? Well, he can't say cause his mouth's so full of meatballs he looks like a squirrel with a chew of tobacco in his cheek.

It took awhile but I finally figured out who that little pooch looked like as I carried him in my coat pocket all the way down to Lions Park. Uncle Ed. Sure as a Polaroid. Uncle Ed—especially when the little fella's mouth is full of meatballs. So that's what I named him—Eddie.

My Uncle Ed was a farmer for all of his life, and he always used to smile and chew Mail Pouch and spit out onto his beanfield during the days leading up to harvest. He'd spit on them for luck. He was proud of those bean-fields like a king of his kingdom, so proud I thought he'd explode. He only had about seventy-five acres and all of that was mortgaged up to his hip boots, but he was proud and he put in hours like you wouldn't believe. He kept the faith and was cocky as the Chrysler man. Most folks who've never farmed don't know what work is. I didn't until I did it. Uncle Ed knew, and so did I for the five seasons I worked for him after I left home. Twelve-hour days, sometimes fifteen.

When uncle Ed's place got collected on, he was never the same. He tried to work in town, but he just couldn't do it. I never saw him smile again, and he died six months later. I know it was cause of the farm. A man's got to have something to work toward, something to build on. When he lost his land, he didn't have nothing to hang onto. With uncle Ed gone, I packed up a few things and headed west and got as far as here. Seems like everybody's here already.

And Eddie's been with me for months now. He's some kind of pal. He'll fetch and growl when somebody's coming and I'm asleep. He's saved me from a rude awakening more than one time. Even when I thought about checking into the mess hall on Bonanza, I knew they wouldn't take Eddie. So hell with them I figured. Eddie's my friend and they're just guys with free food. This is a place you need a friend.

Don't get me wrong. This is a pretty good place, a great place if it didn't have hell's weather. It'd be a better place if I could find a steady job. I work hard, but this ain't exactly farming country, and I don't have the skills most other jobs take. They got no beanfields here, and I wasn't much but trouble before then. I'm not too good at serving up coffee, gambling's not my game, and I didn't have money for rent so my clothes are always slept in. And here I am.

Las Vegas is a good place, but you need a job you can do, especially if you drink. You need a job. It gives you something, like Eddie gives me. It's been more than a year here, and I'm thinking about heading back to Richfield

or out to the Coast or maybe New Mexico. Maybe. But
right now I'd settle for finding my dog, Eddie.

Dark Corner

He woke the other morning with the bad sweats. There was something very wrong this time. The sheets were soaked, his T-shirt drenched in his own heavy musk and something else.

He'd been dreaming again. As usual, the dream floated just outside his consciousness. It was a name and face he could not quite place.

The powerful scent of his sweat filled his nostrils, and in a moment he grew nauseated as he remembered what it smelled like.

Fear.

He hated the stench so much he showered twice to wash it off. It was acrid and foul like spoiled meat. To him, fear smelled like death.

While his head was under the shower, he closed his eyes and instantly returned to the ring. He heard the crowd's roar blend with the rushing water, and in his mind he landed a right hand so flush he could feel his opponent's cheekbone give way.

The ring dream was a snapshot. It came and went flashbulb quick and always melted into self-loathing and the long list of the opportunities he had missed and all the things he had not done with his life.

He was an Olympic finalist with one of those amateur records, seventy-eight wins and one loss, that was as deceiving as it was promising. The truth is, most amateurs can't fight a lick, and half of them wouldn't be there if their daddies hadn't forced them to lace up the gloves. He knew that and could immediately see the fear in their eyes. He was bigger, stronger and quicker than most of his opponents, and he found that he liked to inflict pain, and so the wins came easily.

At first, turning pro was no harder. He beat a string of tomato cans and rapidly rose to No. 9 in the world.

Although he seldom read the gushing sports stories that chronicled his rise, he loved scanning the headlines for his name. He judged whether he liked a story by the size of the headline.

"Bad as they come," an especially good one had declared. "The next Sonny Liston," another shouted.

But the sportswriters didn't know he was so drunk in two of those fights that if the bums he'd been punching hadn't been so weak, he might have toppled over without so much as a slap.

He suffered from bad luck in his first loss. The judges robbed him in his second. The third time he was defeated, the referee stopped the fight too soon. He told himself he hadn't really been out on his feet.

But by then the losing was coming easier. He ballooned to more than 250 pounds and stopped showing up at the gym when his third manager dumped him for a young prospect.

He became a sparring partner for contenders and worked in the ring with two champions to make enough money to keep himself in dope, but after a few months he couldn't hide it. Punctuality was never his strong suit, and a heroin habit is a demanding mistress.

After the Athletic Commission revoked his license, he turned to bouncing for a couple of connected guys who owned a bar and lounge with a bandstand and dance floor. Beating up drunks was easier than the Golden Gloves.

From there, he began running down Charlie Gale's late-paying customers. Truth is, the work was easy and he enjoyed watching the rabbit-scared eyes of the cabbies and casino dealers who had accepted Charlie's money on terms—5 percent a week juice and don't be late—as they recognized his face from the sports pages of their minds. They stammered as they reached for their wallets, or pissed themselves with fear.

And all the while he was using.

Could no one but him tell?

For the longest time he didn't dream at all, but lately he'd been having vivid Technicolor visions of his time in the ring. Not the losses, but the easy victories.

They were so realistic, like a highlight film that played over and over in his head. Everything was right but the minute between rounds. That was where the trouble started.

His trainer wasn't the ornery old Italian who had barked at him for so long and had spent a fortune trying to save his career. It was bigger and darker.

No matter how many times he had the dream, it always ended with the shadow corner man putting his big, black hands on his shoulders, telling him in a voice as deep as a well, "You gonna quit now? You gonna quit now?"

"No," he heard himself say, "I'll never quit. Never."

It was then he would wake up, his body pouring sweat, fear sizzling his senses and stinking up the motel room.

After the second shower, he sat punchy and drained on the edge of the bed. A few minutes passed before he finally realized the identity of the shadowed face from his dreams. It was Sonny Liston calling from the dark corner.

"Sonny Liston," he said to no one but himself, "what you doing calling me?"

CONSTRUCTION

The work was good in Vegas. There was plenty of it, and the weather rarely interrupted the jobs. That's what Carlos liked most when he thought about traveling to Vegas, the work.

It's what had drawn him from Baja Norte, past the border, up through Southern California, and across the Mojave Desert. He'd come into the United States before September 11 when the border security was more relaxed. Even after, he'd seen little change in the flow of people from Mexico to Vegas, and he'd learned through conversations with newcomers that the border crossing had become only slightly more complicated. The easiest way to cross was still to obtain the proper paperwork to enter the United States for a weekend, then simply disappear into the fast-moving landscape. And a country so big that relied that heavily on automobile travel was easy to navigate without being noticed.

"Act like you know what you're doing and where you're going, and watch plenty of television," his cousin, Hector, had told him. Hector had danced back and forth across the border like a coyote. "In America, everyone must act like they know what they're doing and where they're going. And everyone talks like television. It is a good way to learn the language."

And so Carlos went north with a group of other young men who had no difficulty crossing the border or meandering their way to Las Vegas and the promise of plentiful construction jobs. When they arrived, they split up. Carlos had an address of an apartment in North Las Vegas where Hector lived with four other men. The men shared the two-bedroom apartment in a four-plex that was home to an eclectic sample of local society. Carlos looked forward to seeing a friendly face after a month on the road.

He arrived early in the day to the address and waited under the shade of a fruitless mulberry for Hector to return from work. While he sat and thought about what his mother and three sisters were doing back in Tecate, he noted the residents of the complex. Behind one door he heard the chattering of a typewriter and once caught a glimpse of a large, fat man in a bathrobe smoking a cigar as he peered out his smoky window. There was an alcoholic old woman who yelled at children who'd long since grown up and moved away, and a methamphetamine-dealing biker, his skinny girlfriend and their four-year-old girl. The girl's name was Tiffany, and she played in the weed patch side yard by herself for most of the morning, wandering back inside long enough to get a drink of water and receive what must have been a scolding delivered by her mother in machine-gun English. The man of the house came home for a few minutes, roaring up on a smoking, chopped Harley. He passed the parking lot and parked the bike outside the front door of the apartment. The bitter smoke of its exhaust mixed with another chemical scent, one Carlos did not recognize as brewing meth venting through open windows and black-out drapes. It smelled as if something awful had spilled, and Carlos thought about the little girl, who was the age of his sister, Maria Iris.

Loud rock music played for a while, and there was shouting from inside the apartment. The girl went outside with her doll and played in the yard a while longer, and the man on the motorcycle left a short time later.

The warm air and lack of food that morning made Carlos tired, and so he slept under the shade of the fruit-less mulberry. He fell into a dream of his family's home outside Tecate. His father had worked in a Saltillo tile factory for many years and often came home with hands red from the clay. He made little money, but the family was happy and lived a simple, God-fearing life together for many years. It was a place filled with the smells and tastes of his mother's cooking. He swore he could smell her beans cooking in the pot for miles around. He smiled at the thought of her forming the tortillas like little white sheets of sunshine in her hands.

He awoke with a start and found himself staring into the pale blue eyes of the bone-skinny little girl, who stared down at him. He smiled at her. She was a little flower of a child.

Then Carlos heard her mother's voice, jagged as glass.

"Tiffany Baker, get away from that Mexican," she called. "You don't know where he's been."

Big Bill in Spring

Standing in line at the Smith's Food King, barely an arm-load of items in his cart, Big Bill was daydreaming again.

He didn't need the shopping cart anymore. Hadn't for years since his wife had left him and taken the kids to Minnesota, but the truth was he liked to push it around the store and smile at people as he shopped.

Now he was in line, and at his age he had learned to be patient with lines. It was a lesson that appeared lost on the sleep-deprived cocktail waitress standing in front of him with a cart brimming with processed food and two young children dangling from either arm. As she stood before him, something about her looked familiar.

With a tangle of carts ahead of him, there was time to slip into the sort of waking reverie that seeped into his veins this time of year. The days were getting longer, and the weather warmed his old bones and made his gnarled dealer's hands ache a little less from arthritis. Social Security and hotel pensions being what they are, he still put in two shifts a week at a downtown grind joint, taking home a hundred dollars on a good night but averaging more like forty five in tokes. There was a time in his life a hundred had been glorified tip money, but no more.

Like most people his age, he spent his days nursing his bankroll and arguing with Medicare providers who cheated their customers far more often than the shadiest Vegas casino ever had. He watched a little television, read a few paperback novels, thought about the life he'd once had when the mob ran the town.

Life was sweet then. Joy and the kids were still with him. Tokes were fat and the IRS hadn't sunk its fangs into the action. They had a nice four-bedroom ranch-style home in Paradise Valley.

Joy was like a flower in his big hands. Even after the kids she managed to stay slim, her willowy shoulders freckled from the sun. In the early years, he liked to tell her she smelled like sunshine itself.

Big Bill was on top of the world. In those days, he was a hulking fellow with a broad back shaped like a yield sign and powerful arms. He was the sort of man who is so big that people misinterpret his intentions, but Big Bill was no tough guy. Straight off the farm, he was carefree and swore he'd never leave Las Vegas, and he never did.

As every champagne Charlie learns, the party never lasts. It took a few years, for Big Bill had the constitution of a draft horse, but he got carried away with life on swing shift, drinking and partying until dawn after knocking off work at Caesars. Then he started drinking before work. Eventually he missed shifts because of his boozing.

He was bitter for a long time after he got fired, for in those days there was no better job for a card mechanic than those found through inside contacts at Caesars Palace.

He found other work, lost other jobs, never stopped drinking.

After a half-dozen failed attempts, Joy finally got fed up with Big Bill. She packed the kids into the Cadillac and left him a week before Christmas, driving straight into the worst storm in Minnesota in half a century. He never saw them again.

Big Bill responded to what he called her desertion the way he handled everything in those days, by buying a half-gallon of Canadian Club and a bottle of club soda.

If took a few years, but he finally bottomed out. Got some help. Joined AA. Lost so much weight his old drinking friends didn't recognize him. And the fact was, he wasn't the same person. Not really.

These days, he never even dreamed of booze. But he did dream of Joy. He was doing just that as he stood leaning on his cart in line at the supermarket. Her sunshine smell filled his senses, and crazy as it sounds he swore he could see her.

Big Bill reached out into his dream and touched Joy's soft, brown shoulder.

"Honey," he said, "I wanted to tell you how sorry I am for getting lost in Las Vegas."

The woman standing in line in front of him, who was not Joy but a single mother with a devastating case of the graveyard shift wobbles, shook him from his reverie.

"Watch it, freak," she said.

Cathy's Clown

Like so many Las Vegas affairs, it began as an act of naked capitalism. Nothing wrong with that. Nice work if you can get it. Fast money, no exchange of fluids. A little tease, a little green, a quick getaway. A clean transaction.

You want fast money in this town, baby doll, you'd better be prepared to show your tits. Two guns ain't no robbery. That's the name of the game.

Tits are a metaphor, and in this instance a living metaphor. Cathy had them, that was obvious from an early age even before she turned them into a cottage industry.

In case you haven't noticed, money is God here. God, the devil and Kirk Kerkorian all piled into one large bankroll. Please don't call the corporate lawyers. Kirk Kerkorian is a metaphor in this story. We're all metaphors when you stop and think about it. I don't mind that so much; I only wish I knew the meaning of my metaphor.

But back to tits. A crude term, perhaps, but an accurate one. Nursing mothers have breasts and bosoms. Secretaries and store clerks have boobs. Vegas girls have tits.

Like a second set of arms, they earn and earn for the lucky girl and her boyfriend/pimp and provide ample cash to prop up his faulty gambling theories, cocaine jones, and wife and snot-nosed kids on the east end of town. Turns out his wife doesn't understand him, but you do. You and your twin moneymakers and crystal-worshipping soul.

In addition to being metaphors, we're all witches, too. Metaphors and metaphysics; that's the name of the game. The object: to generate money like a living, breathing U.S. Mint.

With the right set and setup, there's plenty of money. Never enough, that much is a given here, but plenty of play cash.

Cathy loved the ease with which she slipped into the night world with her pretty young face and her perky passports. Doors opened. Men and boys drooled. For a while, she received what felt like respect.

She was a handsome girl, to be sure, but the truth was she was no cover girl. Try as she might with makeup and obsessive grooming, her face would never turn heads on Main Street.

Her body was something to behold. As the slapstick goes, "And we was duh boys tryin' to behold it."

Truth is, we didn't stand a chance. As a nightcrawling teenager with bad hair and bitter dreams, I still didn't understand the game. I thought I did, but I was a clueless little fool who courted trouble. I envied Cathy in that regard. She knew what she wanted.

Like me, she was a kid searching for salvation on the banks of the river Styx. But she seemed to understand where she was going whether in class at our high school or after dark working as a break-in dancer, a veritable colt in a G-string and pumps, at a topless joint owned through a proxy by old man Vito of the Bonanno crime family.

This was a long time ago. It's something I did while you were watching "Laverne & Shirley" and nothing I'm proud of. All the people but me are gone now, and that's why I'm telling the story.

I remember the first day after she started dancing for Vito's people. She was late to government class, and I saw she'd been up all night. She was seventeen, and a seventeen-year-old has seemingly infinite reserves of energy. She was stoked, sober and wanted to talk to me after class.

I was only too happy to oblige. I loved Cathy from the first moment I saw her in junior high, but without knowing it I'd passed over into the awful nightmarish netherworld of the male friend. It was a role I hated and would fight mightily against, but it was also one I was willing to accept on the way to the inevitable bliss I fantasized of sharing with her.

"J.L.," she said close to me in the noisy hallway. "I got the job."

She opened her purse. It was full of singles and fins, maybe eighty dollars in all.

"Where, the bank?"

"No, silly, at the Pony."

"The Pink Pony?"

"Yeah, what else? They took a look at my fake ID and hired me right away. Gave me three swings and two graves. I had to kick in some money to the people who run the place, but that still left me with plenty."

I wish I could have frozen that moment in time. When I think back, the melody of her sweet girl's voice whispering "plenty" still rings in my ear.

• • •

Little Jimmy Chili is gone now, thank God, and don't think I didn't wish him dead a thousand times before his corpse turned up, piece by piece, a few miles outside Searchlight some years back. "Topless owner's head found," the indelicate newspaper headline read.

It seems coyotes had been chewing on it. Probably got sick and wisely decided against completing their meal. It couldn't have happened to a nicer slice of Sicilian sleaze, if you ask me.

Little Jimmy's strength at the Pink Pony came from Old man Vito, the aging Bonanno family capo. He owned a couple of used car lots, three pizza parlors, points in a couple of downtown casinos and enough raw real estate to accommodate his own desert island nation. Good help being hard to find, the old man relied on little Jimmy to operate the Pink Pony.

True to his nature, Jimmy was a real asshole about it. I was a kid then and was obsessed with trying to protect Cathy, the love of my young high school life. She'd caught on quickly after landing a dancing job at the Pony with under-the-radar ID.

"You worry too much, J.L.," she told me between classes. Summer was almost upon us that year, and the noon heat already broke one-hundred. It was going to be a miserable summer, I could tell.

"Somebody has to worry about you," I told her. "You know what that place is all about?"

"Money, and a lot of it," she said. "I'm not busting my ass as a busgirl or hustling cocktails like my mom. In and out with a clean getaway. The way I see it, I'll be set for college with a car and condo by the time I'm twenty-one."

"You don't mind if I come by and check on you, do you?"

"Just make sure you bring your lunch money, big boy," she said in her passable Mae West, "or I won't show you my tits."

She squeezed my hand. I noticed her nails had been professionally manicured, Corvette red, and a slender gold watch wrapped her wrist.

"A gift?" I asked.

"From management," she said.

"Management" meant one thing. Cathy was getting to know Jimmy, the hard-case errand boy. In my youthful naiveté, I thought I could help her and fantasized about punching out the little ferret and have Cathy all to myself. My busboy job at the Nevada Hotel paid little, but enough to allow me to sit and drink a beer and watch Cathy dance for the older men, who were mostly polite and only occasionally tried to paw her. She took it all with surprising good nature, as if she'd been dealing with horny drunks her whole life. When our eyes first met, though, I think she was more embarrassed than I was. By the second night, she was smiling at me and winking at me as if we were in this together. But the curtain had come down between us. It's the curtain that emotionally separates dancers from customers.

She'd bring a beer for me and visit between sets on the shadowed stage, and little Jimmy noticed immediately. He spoke to me only once in the weeks I came to the Pink Pony, and I'd like to say how I, as a seventeen-year-old kid, stared down the menacing little Mafia hoodlum and spat out a bit of snappy patter worthy of Bogart or Raft. But the truth is, I was scared to my guts.

"Here he comes, it's Cathy's clown," Jimmy Chili said, his sharp little teeth flashing in the bad light.

All I could do was smile meekly.

Not only was I scared, I knew he was right.

• • •

The world was changing on the last night I saw Cathy work at the Pink Pony. She had hit her stride, had begun semi-dating Jimmy Chili and as a result was working the prime shifts, nights and customers. That meant money. Even in the late 1970s, that meant plenty of money for a seventeen-year-old kid. Enough to get in way over her head.

Cathy had stopped bothering to attend the high school classes we shared. She rationalized it, and so did I for a while. Hey, she was plucking two hundred a night and more from the pockets of the suckers who dropped into the Pink Pony and fell under her spell.

"Don't worry about Jimmy," Cathy told me after me quasi-confrontation with the little gangster. "I'll talk to him for you. It will be fine."

But I wasn't sure. Chili sent one of his goons to sit down next to me and scare the crap out of me, and the dead-dog stare routine worked. I took a deep breath of the sensationally sinful atmosphere, finished my over-priced beer and walked out before I caught an elbow to the head and was carried out by one of the biker-cum-linebackers who hung like apes around the place.

The next day I was approached by a couple of neatly trimmed young fellows in gray sport coats with pressed navy slacks. They were from the FBI and they wanted to know what I was doing to Jimmy Chili that made him so mad.

"Nothing," I told them. "I just know one of the girls who works for him. She goes to my school and we're friends, and he's seeing her. That's all. It's no big deal."

"Your girlfriend got a name?"

I told them and started to sweat. Maybe they knew about the money she'd loaned me that I had loaned several classmates at five percent interest a week. Maybe they knew about the pot or the lack of regular attendance.

I was pretty simple back then. I didn't realize they were trying to work an angle on Jimmy Chili. I would have helped them if I could, but I was just a kid who was swimming in over his head.

"Cathy's a good kid," I said. "She's just a girl."

They smiled and nodded.

Two days later, Cathy was in the hospital. She refused to see me or anybody but her rat mother. I went to the hospital several times and even went into her room, but it was no use. She was always asleep under heavy sedation.

I suspected her boyfriend was behind it, but it wasn't exactly difficult detective work. A week after Cathy went to the hospital, Jimmy Chili disappeared. The FBI and local cops questioned Old Vito and all his boys, but no one knew anything. In those days, street guys still had a little self-respect.

A month later, thanks to a playful coyote, Jimmy Chili's skull rolled up close enough to the highway to be spotted by hikers. The manager of record of the Pink Pony turned up piece by piece, and I was happy as hell. Except when I thought about Cathy.

She disappeared for three or four years, and my life changed after high school. I wound up going to college and working a few projects. I never went back into the Pink Pony, as I've always believed it was bad luck.

I saw Cathy just once, running into her late downtown on Fremont Street in the heart of the motel stroll. I was working on a project and she was still chasing her theory about getting a few bucks ahead so she could quit the business, buy a condo and go to college. She talked about leaving the life any day now, which by then I knew would never come. She had a nasty meth habit and was losing her teeth.

She was so different from the high school princess I'd had the horny hots for, the girl I followed like a one-eyed bloodhound after a panther's scent.

We wound up back at her motel room for some uninspired exercise, and she worked without taking off her bra. When I asked her why, she told me some story, but by then I knew the truth. Jimmy Chili, fearing she might snitch on him, cleaved her nipples and burned her breasts with lit cigarettes. Old man Vito, hearing of his insanity and knowing that he'd never hold up under the pressure that was descending, made him disappear.

Some of Cathy's scars were visible. I averted my eyes.

"You'll always be my high school fantasy," I said after pulling on my clothes.

"You were always a nice guy, Jasper, but I've never known what to do with a nice guy," she said. She'd probably repeated the line to herself a thousand times.

She volunteered to get together soon, after work or on her day off, which meant away from our hooker-John dynamic, and I said that sounded like a plan. We both knew we were lying, but let it hang there in the musty motel room like cigarette smoke.

"It's funny seeing you again. It feels like I'm back in high school," she said, smiling with her bad teeth.

I think she meant it as a compliment.

NEON CHEESE

Robert Fortunato was a gold-chain gangster who liked to call himself Bobby Fortune. Thought it made him sound sexy and mysterious, and everyone knows how a certain brand of woman has an affinity for bad guys.

He played the role with the same zeal Jolson sang "Toot toot Tootsie, Goodbye." He liked to misquote The Godfather and talk about how he knew people. People in New York, people in Chicago, people in K.C., people in Cleveland.

Bobby was what some people call a leaner. That is to say, he would lean into conversations when he thought he had a physical advantage. The menacing posture helped with his reputation as a mob associate, or "some sort of Mafia guy" as the cocktail waitresses who were forced to serve him would sigh.

Some sort was right.

Oddly enough, Bobby came from good stock. He had two uncles with the Office, as the Angiulo brothers' Boston headquarters was known in the days before wiretaps and man-sized rats turned their thing into a vaudeville skit. He liked to brag that he was sent to Las Vegas to help with "the family business," which impressed the neophytes and starry-eyed topless dancers but didn't change the fact he was considered a motor-mouthed nuisance on the street.

He moved money for some broken-down bookmakers and a couple of times hoodwinked some casino dealers into letting him take off their tables and split the proceeds, but he wasn't much of a wiseguy.

Of course, for many years a scuffler need not have been much of a deep-thinker to earn a living on the street in Las Vegas. Anyone with fifth-grade math skills and a menacing glare could lend money for a living, and Bobby's reputation as a connected guy was enough to ensure gambling bum cabbies and blackjack dealers came up with enough weekly juice to keep him in silk shirts, Italian shoes and champagne in a bucket in the corner of the local discos.

In a way, Bobby Fortunato had it made and enjoyed a much better life than any of the real McCoys on the street. They were harassed and followed twenty-four hours a day by Metro intelligence detectives, FBI agents and a few sharp IRS CID operatives. The real thumpers and shooters, extortionists and arsonists had it bad. Sooner or later, they were going to take big falls or dirt naps.

Bobby, conversely, was more likely to get cold-cocked for pinching a cocktail waitress than beat up by one of the sheriff's apes or whacked by a rival gang member. He was living large and lucky for the longest time.

But all good things must end, as they say, and so too it was with Bobby Fortunato's long reign as a Champagne Charlie the Blade.

It started with a phone call. A series of calls, in fact, because Bobby ducked the first two dozen messages left on his apartment answering machine.

The calls started out almost pleasant. They came from his cousin Vitorio, or Little Vic as he was known back home. Little Vic was with serious people and was rumored to be getting made before Christmas. His papa, Big Vic, has been a soldier for thirty years. Which meant he'd spend twenty-four of those years in the penitentiary, but still maintained contact with the street through his son.

Big Vic was one of the people Bobby Fortunato liked to tell square citizens he knew. Big Vic was a killer and, as everyone who watches movies knows, killers are very mysterious and exciting people until you get to know them. The problem for Bobby, of course, was that he really didn't know Big Vic. Even an unlucky mug like Big Vic would never speak to a wannabe like Bobby. In truth, he only knew Little Vic, but over time he'd blended the two men into one story. It worked for Bobby. Especially since he was in Las Vegas, almost three thousand miles from the Office and a crew of wolf-hungry men who would have pimped him out in two seconds just for the bankroll in his tailored pockets.

Over the course of a few weeks, the calls from Little Vic grew increasingly anxious. He'd gradually gone from light-hearted greetings to "Look you stupid sonofabitch" and worse in recent days.

Bobby's reason for ducking the calls was simple: Real-deal wiseguys never phoned to talk about old times.

So, you can imagine how he cursed himself when he accidentally picked up the phone and, expecting to hear from Judy, the cute little thing from the Stardust, heard the voice of his cousin, Little Vic.

"Hey, Bobby," Little Vic growled. "I thought you was dead."

The phone felt heavy in Bobby Fortunato's small hand.

"I hear you been having some fun," Little Vic said, but even one as dense as Bobby knew the small talk was about to end. "It's a good time there, right?"

"It's all right, Vic," Bobby said. "I was about to call you."

"What a coincidence," Little Vic snarled. "I've been calling you for weeks now, and I catch you on the phone and were about to call me. Wait until my old man hears this. He'll laugh his ass off."

"How is he, anyway?"

"He's lonely, Bobby," Little Vic said. "He's lonely because some people he knows and trusts aren't staying in touch and paying their respect. He thinks maybe they don't think of him enough, that maybe they think he's dead and buried in the ground, that maybe they're batting out of their league because they think he can't reach from solitaryfriggingconfinement and crack their ungrateful heads with a ball bat any time he wants to. He thinks that. What do you think about that?"

Bobby's heart did a Buddy Rich drum solo in his chest. His eyes darted around his apartment, which was done up to match a suite he'd once seen at the Aladdin. His guts were turning to water.

"I don't think that's right," Bobby said. "I've been working, been having troubles of my own out here with a couple of projects I got going, but it's coming together. It's just taking me longer to get settled and catch a break.

Plus I had pneumonia for more than a month. I thought I was down for the count."

"You don't start kicking in and kicking up and you might end up with a head cold NyQuil won't cure."

"Now Vic, I swear I got plenty of things going. It's just taking me longer to put together, that's all."

"So how come you haven't kept in touch with your cousin Artie? He tells me he hasn't seen or heard from you in months."

"Come on, Vic, Artie's a pizza man. What am I going to do for him, roll out some dough and slice a pepperoni? I'm looking around. I've got some big things working. I just need a little more time, is all."

"That sounds, what did my lawyer say the other day, oh yeah. That sounds very nonspecific, Bobby. Very, very nonspecific. So nonspecific that I got to ask you a question: Do you really want me to go back to my papa, who spends every minute of his life locked up like an animal, and tell him something this nonspecific? Is that what you want? I don't think you want that, Bobby. In fact, I'm telling you as your old friend that you don't want me to go back to him and tell him that."

"No, you're right," Bobby Fortunato said, the perspiration soaking his tailored silk shirt. "I don't want that. I just need a day or two and I'll have a couple answers for you. Can you give me a day or two?"

"A month ago when I reached out for you and got nothing but your answering machine, then I could give you a day or two. But your day or two turned into six weeks of this nonspecific stuff. Well, the time's come to figure out why we sent you to Las Vegas, other than to spend some seed money and drink that good champagne you've been buying."

They'd been watching him, after all. He knew now it was useless to lie.

"All right," Bobby said. "What do you want me to do?"

"I want you to see your cousin Artie. I'll try to remember not to tell him you called him a pizza man. I don't think Artie would like that. I think he's proud to own eight pizzerias and the Twilight Lounge. He's proud, and he shows a ton of respect for people. You could learn a lot from your cousin, Bobby."

And that is how, three hours later, Bobby Fortunato found himself in the kitchen of the Art of Pizza number three, talking in hushed tones to his diminutive cousin, who was up to his elbows in an enormous pot of ground pork, blending spices and working the fatty meat the way a sculptor works his clay. While Bobby stood by, silently cursing the flour he'd gotten on his slacks, he listened as Artie told him the ingredients in the makings for his locally famous sausage.

"Fennel, plenty of fennel and pour in a little red wine," his cousin Artie was saying. "See, Bobby, it's the little things, like these little fennel seeds, that make the difference. You got to pay attention to details. Come back here tomorrow, and don't wear that wiseguy stuff in here again. This ain't no movie. This is business."

With that, Artie removed his right hand from the vat of pork and took Bobby's in a vice grip that cracked his knuckles.

"We understand each other?"

• • •

Cousin Artie was old school in the extreme. His Art of Pizza restaurants were popular in part because he was old school. While most of his customers showed the usual mediocre taste in Italian cuisine by ordering cheese pizzas and spaghetti, Artie took pride in being able to make just about anything for just about anyone.

His attention to detail got under Bobby Fortunato's collar immediately.

"It's the details," he said over and over in the kitchen, the flour flying and the scent of tomato and olive oil permeating the air. "Life is all about details."

"When do I get to go to work, cousin?" Bobby asked. By work, he meant criminal activity.

"Work? Oh, Bobby, Bobby. This is your work. It's your work to concentrate on the details. Take these two orders. One is for pollo alla Cleopatra, the other for pollo parmigiana. Same chicken breast, two very different dishes."

The two men each held boneless, skinless chicken breasts in their hands.

"Feel the breast, the texture. This is not frozen. This is fresh. Most customers cannot tell the difference, but good customers, the ones who pay attention to details, they can tell.

"For pollo Cleopatra, you take the de-boned breast, give it a good coating of flour and saute in a hot pan with olive oil. Three minutes each side, no more. Take the green onions, the tarragon, one tablespoon fresh, and cook for five minutes. Watch closely how the color of the green onions changes to tan. Smell the tarragon. Feel the dish coming to life. Use your senses, Bobby. Take the salt and pepper and season to taste.

"In a few minutes, add the white wine, the brandy, some heavy cream and some chicken stock. Simmer and reduce. This is very nice, delicate.

"It's all in the details."

Bobby was turning red in the face. In the two weeks he'd been working at his cousin's side, he'd learned to knead pizza and bread dough, cooked a hundred gallons of tomato sauce, cleaned enough calamari to clog the Amalfi Coast. Every time he'd asked about helping his cousin with a project outside the restaurant he'd been told to be patient, to focus on what was in front of him, to never let his mind wander to things in life that were not important.

What Bobby did not realize, or perhaps was of an intellect too inferior to understand, is that his cousin was attempting to school him in the ways of their family's private business. If he couldn't learn to spin a pizza, if he couldn't tell the difference between two chicken dishes, how could he be trusted for anything more important?

Alas, to Bobby cousin Artie made little sense and was too much in love with his kitchen to ever do any real work like one of the real gangsters he'd grown up watching on Federal Hill and at the local movie theater.

As he stood shoulder to shoulder with his cousin, ruining his manicure in the process, Bobby felt like screaming.

Instead, he asked quietly in the middle of Artie's dramatic recitation of his favorite quick pollo parmigiana recipe—"Use the toothpicks to keep the pollo nice and snug and don't forget to sprinkle paprika and the almond slivers with a little fresh Parmesan for luck"—"What does a pan of parmigiana have to do with being a wiseguy?

"No disrespect, cousin, but all these recipes are haunting my frigging dreams at night. This chicken, that veal, pasta and gravy and peas. Help me out here, Artie, I'm begging you. Don't give me any more recipes, or my head will explode.

"The people we both know asked me to come here and help you out. So I'm here helping you out. I've got nine things working and I drop them flat just to come stand here and stick my hands in gnocci and ravioli. I swear on my family I don't get it. I'm doing the work here, but I didn't move to Vegas to become the pizza king."

Bobby knew he had said too much, but there was no taking it back. He watched his cousin's eyes for a sign of emotion and saw nothing in their flat darkness. Although not the most perceptive of men, Bobby noticed that the kitchen, which had four other cooks and helpers, was so silent he could hear the tomato sauce bubbling in the heavy pot on the stove.

"No 'mi scusi,' no 'scusa,' my young cousin. No grazie mille,' no 'prego' or 'per favore.' Are you sure you're not Irish? Non capisco, Bobby. You want to talk with disrespect to your cousin, you're making a mistake. You want to be a wiseguy, you go be a wiseguy. I don't know no wiseguys. I only know the people in my family.

"You want a job to do? Come back here after closing. Until then, I don't want to see your face."

"I understand," Bobby Fortunato said, speaking his biggest lie of all.

• • •

"This is more like it," Bobby Fortunato said to himself as he showered off the scent of the Art of Pizza's kitchen. In the twenty minutes it had taken him to drive back to his high-rise apartment, he had convinced himself that his confrontation with cousin Artie had gone well. "I guess he knows where I'm frigging coming from now," he said with authority as the water's spray washed away the aroma of tomato sauce and bread dough, pan-seared Parmesan and oven-baked mozzarella.

All the good scents from the old world flowed down the drain and were replaced by a gaudy spray deodorant and a flash flood of Paco Rabanne. Bobby had a drink of Chivas, a toot of cocaine, then smoke a few cigarettes as he channel surfed. He was anxious.

Not so much about returning to the Art of Pizza for his first assignment from his cousin, whom he understood through channels was a made guy—but that didn't mean Artie could turn him into a frigging pizza boy. At present Bobby was more concerned about picking the right outfit for whatever lay ahead that evening. He cursed his cousin for not giving him a few details. After an hour, he settled on not wearing a suit.

Instead, he chose a pair of two-hundred-dollar tailored slacks, a simple black pullover and matching sport coat. He looked at his box of rings and selected something not too ostentatious for his pinky.

Then he reached into the bottom of his sock drawer and removed a snubbed .38 with a waistband holster. It fit comfortably on his hip. He had tried it out many times, but had never actually fired it.

Bobby checked his look in the mirror three times, then made sure his nails were buffed to a mirror shine. He very much liked what he saw.

His mood changed considerably when he drove up to the back of the Art of Pizza. Although the alley was not well-lighted, he could see the shadowed figures of three men, none of whom was his uncle. He recognized the two largest men as the "Two Tonys," a pair of twins whose father, who was also named Tony, had played a cruel trick on them by giving them the same name. In Artie's crew, the words, "Hey you, Tony, no, you, Tony" were often heard.

Tonight, the two Tonys didn't speak. Eddie Fusco did.

"You're almost on time, little cousin," Eddie said as Bobby strolled up, reeking of expensive cologne. He'd overshot the wardrobe runway by at least a thousand dollars. The other men were dressed like dockworkers. "Where do you think you're going, the Academy Awards?"

"My uncle told me he had a job for me to do," Bobby said, raising an angular eyebrow at the others. "I didn't know it was digging a ditch."

Eddie Fusco flashed his rat-face smile and said, "That's a good one. Got to remember that."

"Where's my uncle?" Bobby asked, indignant.

"He couldn't make it, so he put me in charge," Eddie replied, nodding to the Tonys and sending them on their way. "We'll take my car."

On the way across town, Eddie presented the plan. It was so simple it infuriated Bobby Fortunato.

"You mean we went through all this to hijack a van full of deli products?"

"That's right," Eddie said, cracking a window and handing Bobby an address written on a piece of paper. "It's easy. In and out. Should take two minutes for you to slip in, grab the van and move. It's all set up. All you have to do is take the one with its lights on. The keys are already in it."

"You got to be kidding me," Bobby said, nonplussed. "It figures this would be the work he wanted."

"I'll try not to remember that," Eddie said, grinning again. "See you at that address on the paper."

Bobby exited the car and brushed himself off. This was a frigging joke, he thought, walking up to the gate of International Cheese Distributors. He walked onto the property, saw two men standing in the distance, noticed no security guards. He quickly moved to the van.

It reeked of heavy Italian cheese, the kind that had filled the deli cases of his youth, the sort his uncle raved over.

Before he got in, he noticed a semi truck idling next to the van. Its lights were also on. It, too, was ready to make a midnight run.

Working quickly, he closed the door of the van and climbed into the semi. The gears were complex, but he jammed the stick and popped the clutch and lurched forward. In no time he was out the front gate and on the road. He dug into his pocket and pulled out the address Eddie Fusco had given him. To his surprise, it was less than a mile from the International Cheese Distributors.

He laughed again.

"I can't wait to see the look on my uncle's face when he sees this," Bobby said, his voice lost in the roar of the diesel.

The big rig Bobby Fortunato steered through the night streets barely squeezed through the front gate of Honest John's Auto Yard. Bobby brought the Kenworth with the refrigerated trailer loaded with freshly stolen goods to a stop. He shut off the big diesel's ignition and cut the headlights.

He hopped out of the cab in front of his cousin Artie and four other men, dusted off his trousers and flashed his hands dealer style, as if to show he'd completed his mission without a hitch.

Bobby Fortunato was not the most observant of men, but he immediately noticed that only his cousin Artie was looking at him. He could tell that much even in the bad light of the scrap yard.

"What do we have here?" his cousin asked.

"You sent me to heist a truck, I heisted a truck," Bobby replied, slightly agitated but thrown off guard by the lack of eye contact from the other men.

"I sent you to pick up a van," Artie said, quietly.

"Right, but then I saw this big frigging Kenworth just idling there. It holds what, twenty times what that little van can hold? It's got to be loaded with everything you need."

His cousin nodded.

"Let's take a look, Bobby, and you tell me what you see," Artie said.

The two men walked to the back of the rig with the others two steps behind. Bobby had difficulty opening the trailer, and was chilled by the blast of cold air.

"See here, it's loaded," Bobby said, grinning confidently.

Cousin Artie continued to nod.

"It's loaded, all right," he said. "Loaded with two tons of shit cheese. Cheese nobody in his right mind would eat. Cheese with no flavor, no character, no nothing. Two tons of American frigging cheese, Bobby.

"Tell me, my simple cousin, do you know what American cheese is good for? Stopping your heart, that's what it's good for."

His stare was hard as stone.

Then Bobby Fortunato made a fatal mistake.

"Come on," he said. "Cheese is cheese."

Artie nearly took a heart attack on the spot. His loyal henchmen murmured to themselves.

"Cheese is cheese?" he snarled. "Cheese is cheese? You don't know Parmigiano from a Pontiac and you're telling me cheese is cheese. What about fontina, you know fontina? No, of course not. You're too busy preening in the mirror to know fontina, or gorgonzola, pecorino, sardo, grana padana or ta leggio. How about Toscano, my stupid cousin? You know Toscano? Cheese is cheese."

With that, Artie the made guy, who was old school and had been told to give Bobby Fortunato one last chance to make something of himself, but, in any case, use his best judgment and do what he thought was best to preserve the family honor and tradition, cast a sidelong glance at one of his men, then nodded so slightly it was barely noticed even from three feet away.

"I don't suppose," cousin Artie said, "that you see any heroin wrapped up like wheels of Parmigiano in here, do you?"

It was then Bobby Fortunato had an epiphany, which was rare for most men but especially so in his case. He realized how stupid he had been to underestimate his cousin, a simple pizza parlor owner who worked fourteen hours a day to make authentic meals at affordable prices.

A moment later, a big right hand thrown by the largest of Artie's men, a former New Jersey amateur heavyweight boxing champion, landed squarely on Bobby's left cheekbone, shattering it like a walnut. From that moment, things rapidly degraded.

"Cheese is cheese," Bobby cried at one point, spitting blood and teeth. "Cheese is cheese."

• • •

Nine days later, acting on an anonymous tip, a Metro patrol car pulled up behind an International Cheese Distributors semi that area workers said had been parked in the back end of a construction parking lot for several days. The keys were in the cab, but there was no sign of a driver.

"Kids on a joy ride," one cop said to his partner. "I'll call it in."

"First let me see what's in the box," the other officer said, pointing to the trailer.

Sliding the big hasp, the cop yanked open the large metal door. The trailer let out a gasp. Its refrigeration unit had been shut off, and the stench from the contents was overpowering.

Cheese, case after case of American and Jack cheese. Atop it all, the badly bloated corpse of a man, his mouth crammed full of yellow mush the consistency of Play-Doh. The stench of his bodily juices mixed with the overwhelming odor of spoiled milk.

Strange, thought one cop, who fancied himself a man of culinary taste beyond his humble means. The combination smelled faintly of a good, aged Parmigiano.

About the Author

John L. Smith is an award-winning columnist with the *Las Vegas Review-Journal* and the author of many books on the city and its characters. In 2013, his newspaper commentary took first place in the "Best of the West" and Nevada Press Association contests. He lives with his daughter in a mountain community just outside the lights of Las Vegas.